The Stars

Entangled
Book 9

Jill Sanders

GRAYTON

The Stars

This is a work of fiction. Names, characters, organizations, places, events, and incidents are either products of the author's imagination or are used fictitiously.
Text copyright © 2024 Jill Sanders
Printed in the United States of America
All rights reserved.
No part of this book may be reproduced, stored in a retrieval system, or transmitted in any form or by any means, electronic, mechanical, photocopying, recording, or otherwise, without express written permission of the publisher.
Published by Grayton Press

Summary

Can a modern-day Pandora and her destined protector save the world from impending chaos before it's too late?

Amy has the worst luck when it comes to love. After being abandoned by her latest boyfriend in the middle of nowhere, she's convinced that happy endings aren't meant for her. It might be the nightmares that have plagued her for years that have been straining her relationships. Or perhaps it's the chaos that seems to follow her everywhere. Whatever the cause, Amy has sworn off men entirely. To make matters worse, she has recently discovered that she is the reincarnation of Pandora. Yes, that Pandora, the guardian of the legendary box containing both the hopes of humanity and the potential for its destruction.

Dante Hicks, a local police officer and keeper of the keys, has always known his purpose. It wasn't until Amy reentered his life that he realized she was the one he was destined to save and protect. However, Amy has done nothing but avoid and torment him. With the world seemingly on the brink of collapse, can Dante persuade Amy to trust him before it's too late?

Prologue

Amy woke with a start. Something wasn't quite right. It was too quiet. Opening one eye, she realized the bed was empty next to her.

"Ryan?" She sat up and stretched her arms over her head.

He stepped inside the door to the hotel room from outside, no doubt having a late-night cigarette. When she looked at him, she knew why she'd allowed him to push her around for the past few months. God, he was gorgeous. The man had everything. Looks and a job that paid well enough that he constantly bought her things. Most importantly, he was her ticket to staying out of her small hometown of Hidden Creek.

Then she noticed the look on his face.

"What's wrong?" She sat up a little more.

"Seriously? You can ask me that?" Ryan shook his head. "Whatever, I'm out of here." He tossed some things quickly into his backpack.

"What?" She blinked a few times. "Why?"

Ryan glanced over his shoulder at her as if she was

crazy. Then he laughed and sighed. "Don't be crazy. I've got to." He slipped on his jacket and glanced at the door.

"You're serious?" she asked, jumping up from the bed.

"And you weren't?" Ryan asked without looking back at her. "Crazy bitch," he mumbled as he slammed the door behind him.

If she'd been paying attention, she would have seen the look of hurt in his eyes as he bolted out the door, leaving her there, stranded. Instead, she watched him go and felt her chances of ever leaving the vortex that was her hometown slip out of her fingers.

Chapter One

It wasn't the first time Ryan had left her stranded. In the short six months they'd been dating, this was the third time she'd had to find her own ride somewhere. This was the first time he'd left her this far from anywhere, though. The other two times, she had been able to take an Uber home.

She doubted that she'd be able to hire a car to drive her to Hidden Creek this far out in the country.

Her luck with men had never been good. She'd believed that Ryan was different. Sure, she hadn't strayed far from her type as far as looks go. She couldn't help but fall for the muscular types. Meatheads. Jocks. She'd believed he was different from all her other boyfriends because Ryan was a runner, not a football player. He'd fooled her.

The fact that he'd called her a crazy bitch, well, that was odd. It wasn't the first time someone had called her bitch or crazy, but both at once? Never.

This was the last time she'd fall for someone like him.

Being stranded at the hotel roughly twenty miles from home was a nuisance. Well, her old home, at any rate. For the past year, she'd called her small one-room apartment in Atlanta home. She hadn't strayed far from where she'd grown up, but at least she had technically been out of Hidden Creek.

She and Ryan had broken things off at least once before. This time, however, when he came crawling back to her, there was nothing he could do to change her mind. The relationship was finally over. Actually, thinking about it, she might just take a break from men altogether.

Why not take a year or two to focus on herself? School had been going great and even though she had to work a stupid job to keep up with her classes, she might just redefine who she was.

Find herself.

For now, however, she had to get back to Hidden Creek somehow.

The next morning, with few other choices, she headed over to the diner across the road from the hotel. Normally, she would have called her brother, since her parents were out of town for a month-long trip to Alaska.

The only reason she worried about calling Joe and his wife Liz to come get her was that they were expecting their first child any day now. That was the whole reason she and Ryan had been heading back to Hidden Creek in the first place. They had planned on staying at her parents' place until her new nephew or niece was born.

Why her folks had planned an extensive trip when their first grandchild was due was beyond her.

Joe and Liz were keeping the gender of the baby a secret, so she'd bought neutral-colored gifts. But they were still in Ryan's car. Good luck getting those gifts back from him. Ryan had also taken off with her purse. Her bad habit of always leaving it in her car stung now.

At least she'd had her cell phone and ten dollars in her pocket, which would pay for her breakfast.

Dressed in her worn jeans and one of Ryan's old college sweatshirts that he'd left behind, she headed across the street to the diner. Her makeup bag had been in the car, so she went without. Her brush was in the same bag, so she tied her long blonde hair in a braid.

It was lucky that she'd decided to head to the diner. She'd still been debating waking Joe up, but knowing he worked at the liquor store that he'd inherited a few years back from their uncle, she'd hesitated.

Then she'd spotted the cute couple sitting at the diner and had overheard them mentioning Hidden Creek. It wasn't that strange, as they were less than twenty miles from the town and, along this stretch of highway, you were either heading towards the small town she'd grown up in or back to Atlanta. A fifty-fifty shot.

Besides, the woman, an Asian beauty roughly her age, kept glancing at her as if she knew her. Had she gone to school with her?

She stood up and instantly felt like sitting back down. But then she locked eyes with the woman and something drew her across the room towards them.

"I'm sorry to interrupt," she said, feeling as if she had no control over her own body, "but did I overhear that you are heading to Hidden Creek?"

"We are," the man answered smoothly, as if they'd been waiting for her.

What was she doing? Why couldn't she turn around and go sit back down?

"I hate to ask, but can I get a ride with you?" she said,

totally shocked that she was asking strangers for a ride. This wasn't like her. "I'm from there and, well, my boyfriend..." She rattled on and rolled her eyes. "Well, now he's my ex. He just broke up with me and left me at the hotel. He even took my purse, and I only had ten dollars in my pocket. I'm Amy, by the way. Amy Reed." Shut up. Why couldn't she just shut up? "My brother Joe owns a liquor store in Hidden Creek. Hidden Creek Wine & Liquor, if you've heard of it. You can look me up. I'm not some crazy woman, I swear." Oh god, this was just going horribly. She felt her face heat as she continued to just vomit words. "I was going to call my brother and have him come give me a ride, but..." She shrugged and glanced out the window wishing she was anywhere but here. Why was she doing this? She always did this. "I didn't want to wake him or Liz up this early in the morning since they work late at the store and, well, Liz is pregnant."

"Why don't you have a seat?" The man motioned towards the spot next to the woman.

"Thanks," she said and, to her horror, she actually sat down.

"I swear Ryan normally doesn't do this. Just up and leave me." She sighed. "Joe's been warning me about the guy for months. I guess he was right." She sagged in her chair. "Gosh, you two are such a cute couple. What are your names?" she asked as she bit her lip. There, that would force her to shut up.

The man motioned to the woman. "This is Mia. I'm Lucas."

"Are you just visiting Hidden Creek?" she asked as she fidgeted in her seat.

"We're... thinking of moving there," Mia admitted.

The Stars

"I actually know your brother," Lucas said, surprising her.

"You do?" Mia and Amy said at the same time.

Lucas smiled and nodded. "I met him the last time I was in Hidden Creek. He helped me with... a problem that I had. We rented a house a few miles from their house," Lucas said.

"Oh, cool." Amy relaxed slightly. The fact that the man already knew her brother made her feel better about barging in on the couple.

For the next half hour, while they waited for her food, they chatted about the town, what each of them did for a living, and how they had met. She found the story of them meeting through a mutual friend very interesting. They left out a lot of details, but Amy didn't mind. She could tell they were in love and far closer to each other than she and Ryan, or any other boyfriend she'd had for that matter, had ever been.

Once they were finished eating, they climbed into Lucas's car and headed towards town. They were about a mile out of Hidden Creek when Mia asked Lucas to pull over.

"What's wrong?" he asked when she jumped out of the car.

Amy worried that Mia was going to be sick. Had she eaten something bad at the restaurant? She knew that bird flu had passed through the state a few weeks back so maybe it was that.

"Are you okay?" Amy asked Mia when she climbed out of the car after her.

"You need to come with me," Mia said, shocking her, then she took her hand and started pulling her through the tall grass. "Trust me."

She frowned over at Lucas, who shrugged. "Let's take a walk," he suggested, and the three of them walked through the field.

"Here." Mia stopped frowning as she did a full circle.

"Wrong time?" Lucas asked.

Mia was glancing up at the sky. "We need to come back," she said finally.

"What's going on?" Amy asked. "Why are we in the Anderson's field?" She knew this field well. Actually, her parents' place was less than a mile from here. If she wanted, she could just walk home.

Lucas turned to her and then did a circle. "Where's the silo?" he surprised her by asking.

"Gosh, you know about that?" Amy smiled. Then she turned and pointed in the direction of the old military silo. It wasn't as if it was a town secret. In the past few years, there had been plenty of stories circulating about strange things happening down there. Some of which included her brother and his wife, along with their new group of friends. "Just over there. Jacob keeps the entrance locked now. We used to go down there and party all the time in school," she admitted.

"We will need the others," Lucas said to Mia. "For now..." He glanced at his watch. "I can text them to meet us at the Harvest Moon Family Restaurant. We just ate, but I bet everyone else would enjoy brunch." Lucas turned to Amy and smiled. "My sister Tara owns the new place."

"Oh, I'd heard that it opened up a few weeks back. I've been out of town for... a while." She shrugged. "I can walk from here," she suggested when they headed back to the car. She didn't want to bother the couple any further.

"No, it's okay. I'll text Joe and have him meet us there too," Lucas said, pulling out his phone.

By the time they'd all climbed back into the car, his phone chimed with her brother's reply.

"They're heading there now," he said to the car.

"Thanks," Amy said and sat back. She was quiet for the rest of the trip, deep in thought about what she was going to tell her brother about being abandoned outside of town.

When they pulled into town, all of the tension Amy had been feeling for the past few hours disappeared.

She hated to admit it, but being home felt right.

When she stepped into the new restaurant, she instantly wanted to make her escape. But a few more people came in and, for some reason, she became too curious to leave. Introductions were made over lunch. Everyone was there.

She knew everyone. Some had grown up in the small town while others were new. She had known Xtina for years and had met her husband Michael at least once before. They had a daughter named Harper.

Brea and Ethan were both new to town. Ethan was Michael's twin. They had a son named Milo.

Both Jess and Jacob were locals and had a son Reed. It had been a shock to find out a few years back that Jacob was Michael and Ethan's older brother, who had been given up for adoption against their parents' wishes when they'd been teenagers. Jacob was the law in town and had taken over for his adopted father a few years back.

There was a woman named Joleen and her husband Mason.

Lucas's sisters, Tara and Selene, were also there with Tara's fiancé Colt and Selene's boyfriend Scott. Selene and Scott were very friendly with Mia and Lucas, while Tara and Colt acted as if they'd only met the couple a few times before.

When Joe and Liz walked in, Amy felt a rush of embarrassment hit her when her brother wrapped his arms around her.

"I'm going to kill him for leaving you stranded," he whispered in her ear. "Later."

She wanted to argue with him, but in truth, she wanted to get her hands on Ryan just as badly.

"I'll let you," she said back.

Tara and Colt had just opened the restaurant, Harvest Moon Family Restaurant, and since neither of them had had a chance to sit down and talk much, she didn't know much about them.

"We don't close for a few more hours," Tara said to the entire group when she stopped by their table to refill everyone's water. "But if you want, we can all meet out at Xtina and Michael's place this evening?"

"That'll do. We want to go check into our rental and maybe have a shower and change," Lucas said.

"Let's say eight?" Xtina suggested.

Amy didn't think their conversation had anything to do with her, so she happily nibbled on the onion rings her brother bought for her while the rest of the group talked about cooking dinner at Xtina and Michael's place.

She planned to get to her parents' place, shower, change into some old clothes that she kept there, and watch an old movie while she ate all the junk food her mother kept hidden around the house.

After they finished their food, they all left and went their separate ways. Joe dropped her off at her parents' place and she took a very long bubble bath and enjoyed her parents' jacuzzi tub and her mother's expensive bath salts and shampoos.

Then she pulled on her thickest and most comfortable

The Stars

pajamas, the ones with the cows all over them, and climbed into bed. Even though it was two in the afternoon, she fell fast asleep.

At first, she didn't realize that she was dreaming. The mist circling her blocked her vision, making her believe that she was in a large room filled with smoke. Her lungs burned with the dampness of the space. Her skin, muscles, and even her bones ached as if she'd been beaten.

All the time she heard water dripping. Slowly. Methodically. Annoyingly.

She was freezing and soaked to the bone.

"Hey," someone whispered. "Are you okay?"

She blinked and a dark figure formed across the space.

Drip. Drip. Drip.

"Hey," the voice came again, sounding more worried.

She blinked and looked up into dark eyes filled with concern. Eyes she oddly knew. Eyes that awakened something deep down in her soul.

A blast of something she'd never felt before caused every fiber of her body to jolt. She screamed and jerked under its power.

"Hey!" Drip, Drip. "Wake up!"

Her eyes jerked open as she sat up, breathless, covered in sweat. Her body shook.

It took her a few moments to get herself back under control. Everything she was wearing was soaked. Either from sweat or... had she been in that damp room? No, that was impossible.

Besides, there was no way that she'd just seen her high school crush, Dante Hicks, standing over her wearing some sort of a gladiator's outfit.

Chapter Two

"Time is relative," Jacob told him as they strolled into the Coffee Corner just past five in the morning.

Winter had yet to fully settle in the south, but it was cold enough that he had on his heavy jacket to ward off the early morning mist. The fog was so thick, it had taken him an extra ten minutes to get to work. Which is why he was getting the lecture from his boss.

"Well, relative or not, when the fog is too thick to even see your hand in front of your face, it's gonna take a little longer to get into work," Dante said as he held the door open for his boss to walk past him.

Jacob chuckled. "You know, you could always head in early?"

"The fog wasn't this thick up the hill," he pointed out. "Besides, breakfast with my boss isn't a requirement for me to keep the job."

Jacob slapped him on the back, hard. "True, but it helps next time you want a day off."

Dante nodded and then waited until Jacob ordered his coffee and food before putting in his standard order.

For the past five years or so, Dante had been working under Jacob. He'd worked under Jacob's old man briefly before he'd retired and Jacob had taken over. He'd known Jacob all his life. The same as he'd known pretty much everyone in his small hometown of Hidden Creek, Georgia.

Fresh out of high school, he and Jacob had started police training and had slipped into their uniforms to serve and protect the town of roughly ten thousand. Many of those residents had been added in the past few years, thanks to all the publicity the town had recently gained.

The police job had allowed him to purchase his cabin home on top of one of the hills overlooking the town. Hidden Creek was nestled in the valley and straddled the actual creek, which ran directly through it like the veins in a heart. Hidden Creek was more than home, it was probably the best place on earth. Or so Dante believed.

Sure, he'd spent most of his hard earned money fixing the place up. Within the first six months, he'd had to replace the metal roof, gut the bathroom and kitchen, and add a new sump pump. Now, however, every time he walked into his home, it was like walking into a dream world. He couldn't remember the last time he'd felt so... right.

Except for that one night at prom during his senior year. For a few short hours, he'd felt the same way. Everything had been as it should be.

While he and Jacob waited for their food, they went over a few details from yesterday's reports. After the food arrived, the topic changed to town gossip.

They were halfway through their breakfast when Jacob mentioned that Amy Reed was back in town. He tried to hide his interest in hearing more, but some-

The Stars

thing told him that Jacob already knew about the lifelong crush that he'd had on her. It was obvious in the way the man talked to him and watched him as he spoke.

"Lay off," he grumbled to Jacob, who chuckled in response.

"Dude, you never laid off me when I was toiling with Jess," Jacob pointed out.

"Toiling?" Dante teased. "You mean avoiding her like the plague."

Jacob laughed, a burst of it echoing in the coffee shop. He glanced over and winked at the woman behind the counter. "She was worth the wait."

Dante glanced over to Jessica St. Clair and agreed with a quick nod of his head.

"Enough about your perfect life," he said, and took a bite of his breakfast muffin.

"Dude, you could have what I have. Just sayin'." Jacob took a sip of his coffee and glanced out the windows. "Speaking of..." He grinned and nodded.

Just outside the large windows, with the mist swirling around her, Amy climbed out of her car and headed towards the door of the coffee shop.

Damn. She looked even better than he remembered. How long had it been since he'd seen her? A year? Two?

Her long sandy blonde hair was past her shoulders and was tied up in a thick braid over her left shoulder. The sweatshirt and sexy black leggings she was wearing had his heart rate spiking.

"You're a goner," Jacob whispered as Amy walked into the door and glanced around.

If she noticed him, she didn't react and instead strolled to the counter and waited to place her order.

"You could grow a pair and go over there and ask her out. Finally," Jacob added with a nudge.

Thankfully, just then both of their walkie-talkies squawked to life.

Dante silently thanked the universe for the timely interruption as he grabbed his radio and placed his breakfast muffin down. Jacob's amused grin didn't go unnoticed as he reached for his own radio, the static filling the air between them.

"All units, we've got a situation near the old mill. Possible break-in. Responding officers needed."

Dante cleared his throat, slipping into professional mode. "Unit 7 responding," he said, keeping his voice steady, though his pulse quickened. Jacob echoed the call and downed the rest of his coffee.

"Saved by the squawk," Jacob teased, already moving towards the door.

Dante shot him a glare, though his heart still raced, not just from the call but from the fact that Amy was only a few feet away, oblivious to the internal storm she was causing him. He didn't have the time or courage to talk to her now. Duty called, and it was far easier to face potential danger than to confront the feelings for Amy that he'd been dodging for years.

As they moved outside into the mist, the early morning chill felt sharper and more invigorating.

The old mill was a couple of miles away on the edge of town, but Hidden Creek wasn't exactly known for major crimes, so this had his curiosity piqued.

"You think it's just kids messing around?" Dante asked as they hopped into the patrol car, the fog making the road ahead look eerie in the early morning light.

"Probably," Jacob said, shrugging. "But you never know

The Stars

these days. The town's changing. Used to be, you could leave your front door open and not worry about a thing. Now we get calls like this every other week."

The engine rumbled to life, and soon they were speeding towards the outskirts of town. Dante couldn't help but glance in the rearview mirror, catching sight of the lit coffee shop sign shrinking in the distance behind them. Amy was still there, and he'd be lying if he said part of him didn't want to turn the car around, walk up to her, and say something—anything.

But that wasn't him. Not now, maybe not ever.

"Hey, you okay?" Jacob asked, his tone slightly less teasing than before. "You were pretty quiet back there."

Dante nodded, gripping the wheel a little tighter. "Yeah, just... thinking about the job."

Jacob snorted. "Right. And by 'job,' you mean Amy Reed."

He shot him a look, but Jacob's grin only widened. "Listen, man. We're not kids anymore. If you want something, you gotta go after it. She's not just gonna wait around forever."

Before Dante could respond, they pulled up to the old mill, the abandoned building looming in the fog. The radio squawked again, filling the silence.

"Unit 7, confirm you're on site."

"Confirmed," Dante replied, stepping out of the car. The air was thick. Maybe it was just the fog or the eerie quiet of the old mill, but something felt... off.

Jacob, ever the optimist, slapped him on the back again. "Come on, let's check it out. Could be nothing."

But as they approached the old wooden door, Dante couldn't shake the feeling that today, "nothing" was exactly what it wouldn't be.

The door to the mill creaked ominously as Dante pushed it open, the rusty hinges groaning in protest. Inside, the darkness swallowed them whole, only the faint beams of their flashlights cutting through the thick gloom. The air was damp and musty, filled with the scent of decay and old wood. Dante's breath felt heavier in his chest, but he chalked it up to the atmosphere—mills like these always had a way of making you feel uneasy.

Jacob stepped in beside him, his flashlight sweeping across the vast, open space. Dust motes floated lazily in the air, disturbed by their entry. The only sounds were the distant creak of wood settling and the muted drip of water somewhere deep within the building.

"This place gives me the creeps," Jacob muttered, his voice echoing softly in the cavernous room. "Reminds me of that horror movie where—"

"Don't start," Dante interrupted, keeping his eyes sharp on their surroundings. His pulse was already thrumming in his ears, and the last thing he needed was Jacob's usual banter to ramp up his nerves. There was something off about this place, something that set his instincts on edge.

As they moved deeper into the old building, the fog from outside crept in through the broken windows and cracks in the walls, giving everything an ethereal, almost haunted quality. Their footsteps echoed against the worn stone floor, each step making the silence feel heavier, more oppressive.

Jacob went left while Dante turned to the stalls on the right. Dante moved towards a large metal structure in the corner, remnants of the mill's machinery. As he approached, his flashlight caught something unusual—a trail of dark stains leading towards the back of the building.

Dante's gut clenched. "What the hell is that?" he whispered as he knelt, shining his light closer. The stain was dark and sticky, like dried blood. "Could be an animal, I guess. Or..." His voice trailed off, and he didn't finish the sentence.

Suddenly, a loud clatter broke the stillness. Dante's heart leaped into his throat as something rushed past them in the darkness. Whatever it was, it was larger than he'd expected. Bigger than he was by double. His first thought was a bear, but the lack of fur threw him off.

The air stirred violently, followed by the sound of heavy footsteps pounding against the floor.

"Shit!" Dante swore, jumping back, his flashlight swinging wildly.

"What?" Jacob said from across the space.

Dante's own light flickered as he caught a glimpse of something large and fast darting into the shadows of the trees a few yards outside the open doors. For a split second, his mind tried to process what he'd just seen—a flash of skin, the glint of sharp eyes—but it was gone before he could make sense of it. His heart was racing now, the adrenaline surging through his veins.

"What the hell was that?" Jacob asked, his voice tight as his light zeroed in on the door, which was now swinging due to the creature who had pushed through it.

"An animal," Dante muttered, but his voice lacked conviction. His pulse thundered in his ears as he scanned the darkness around him for any sign of movement. The thing had moved too fast, too erratically. "Could've been a dog or... maybe a coyote." He tried to convince himself. It for sure wasn't a bear. Not the way it had moved.

Jacob exhaled sharply, regaining his composure. "Yeah. Coyote, probably. They're getting bolder, coming closer to town."

Dante wasn't so sure, but he didn't say anything. Instead, he motioned for them to keep moving, his gut still twisted with unease.

They followed the trail of blood deeper into the mill, where the darkness seemed to thicken around them. The beams of their flashlights trembled as they swept over old machinery, stacks of rotting crates, and broken beams. The place felt like a tomb, and Dante couldn't shake the feeling that something—someone—was watching them.

Then they found it.

The flashlight beams fell on the figure of a goat lying in a twisted heap near the far wall. Its body was mutilated, the fur matted with blood and deep gashes carved into its sides. The sight was grotesque, and the smell hit them seconds later, pungent and coppery.

Jacob grimaced, stepping closer to inspect the body. "Jesus..."

Dante swallowed hard, fighting the wave of nausea that rose in his throat. "Coyotes did this?"

Jacob nodded, but there was doubt in his eyes. "Yeah. I mean... what else could it be?" He poked at the ground near the carcass with the toe of his boot. "It's messy, but coyotes will tear into livestock like this. Especially if they're desperate for food."

Dante stared at the goat, the jagged wounds. The eerie silence had settled over the mill again. Something wasn't sitting right with him. He'd seen coyote attacks before—hell, he'd dealt with a few himself—but this... this was different. The gashes were too deep, too precise. And there was something about the way the animal had been left there like it had been placed on display.

He felt a chill crawl up his spine.

"Let's get this reported," Jacob said, turning to head

back towards the entrance. "We'll call animal control, let them handle the carcass."

Dante nodded, his mind still lingering on the strange attack. As they walked back towards the car, he couldn't help but glance over his shoulder towards the outcropping of trees the creature had disappeared into.

He had a strange feeling that whatever had been in there... wasn't finished.

Chapter Three

Amy took a deep breath, forcing her heart rate to settle as she watched Jacob and Dante disappear through the mist outside. She let out a sigh of relief and leaned against the counter. Despite knowing them both for years, there was something about seeing them in uniform that set her on edge. It wasn't like she was a criminal or anything—far from it—it was full blown attraction. Hard. Fast. Powerful attraction.

Feelings she couldn't afford to have right now. Her hand slid into her jacket pocket, fingers brushing the small bag of weed. Why hadn't she gotten rid of it? That question nagged at her, tugging at the edges of her conscience. It wasn't like she even used it that often. Ryan had been the one to drag her into that scene. Always pushing her to "loosen up" and "have some fun." Now that he was out of her life, she should have just ditched it. Instead, it lingered there, a reminder of a part of her she wished she could just leave behind.

"Everything okay?" Jess's voice snapped her out of her thoughts.

Amy plastered on a smile, even though her heart still raced. "Yeah. Just... you know, old habits."

Jess gave her a knowing look from behind the counter. "Still jumpy, huh? You've gotta relax. I'm telling you, Hidden Creek is about as safe as it gets. Besides, Jacob and Dante aren't exactly the types to go sniffing around for trouble. They've known you forever." Jess touched her hand and then nudged her coffee order towards her.

Amy laughed softly, but it was forced. Jess didn't know about her exes, about the mess she'd been tangled in before she decided to come back home. If she did, maybe she wouldn't be so casual about it. The truth was that Amy had fallen into some bad habits when she left Hidden Creek. She'd been trying to outrun the small-town life, the memories of growing up here, and most of all —Dante.

He'd always been the one that got away. No, not got away—she'd *pushed* him away. Senior prom, the last night she could remember feeling like everything was right. They'd danced, laughed, and even shared a kiss under the string lights behind the gym.

He hadn't called her after that night, but it wasn't as if she had tried too hard to win him over. And right after graduation, she was gone. Off to chase a life that wasn't even hers to begin with.

"Amy?" Jess's voice softened as she wiped down the counter, her brow furrowed with concern. "You're not thinking about Ryan again, are you?"

Amy's stomach twisted at the mention of his name. She bit down hard on the inside of her cheek and shook her head. "No. Not him. Not anymore."

But it wasn't a lie she could sell. Ryan had done a number on her. She knew that much. His rough edges, his

The Stars

recklessness—they had felt exciting in the beginning, but by the end, it was nothing but chaos.

"Good," Jess said firmly, tossing the rag over her shoulder. "Because you deserve way better. And if you're gonna stick around this time, you've gotta stop looking over your shoulder like the sky's gonna fall."

Amy smiled again, this time a little more genuinely. "You're right. I'm fine. Really." She didn't know who she was trying to convince more, Jess or herself.

Jess rolled her eyes, but a grin tugged at her lips. "Well, if you ever want to talk... or need to borrow my dog to walk around town for protection, let me know." She smiled. "And remember, I'm married to the chief of police." She motioned towards the glass. "He may be the boss of the town, but I'm the boss of him."

Amy laughed, the tension finally starting to loosen in her chest. "I'll keep that in mind."

Just then, her phone buzzed in her pocket, vibrating against the small bag of weed. She fished it out, praying it wasn't Ryan trying to weasel his way back into her life. Her heart eased when she saw it was only a notification from her old landlord, telling her that he'd released her from her month-to-month lease.

Thankfully, earlier that morning, she'd managed to secure a short-term rental just outside of Hidden Creek. It was a small cabin by the creek, away from the noise and too many memories of her parents' home.

Her parents were due back home any day now, and she was not going to try and live with them again. Not after last time. She loved her folks, really, but she was twenty-five.

After glancing out the window, her gaze lingered on the fading mist, the place where Dante and Jacob had disappeared just minutes earlier. Her pulse picked up again, not from fear this time, but from something else—something she hadn't felt in a long time. Dante had looked good. Better than she remembered, honestly. Broad shoulders, steady gaze, that easy sexy smile he always flashed her when they were younger.

"Earth to Amy," Jess teased, bringing her back to reality.

Amy blinked and cleared her throat, forcing herself to look away from the window. "Sorry. Just... thinking about how much has changed since I've been gone."

Jess leaned on the counter, a mischievous glint in her eye. "Or maybe thinking about how much someone has changed?"

Amy rolled her eyes, but her cheeks warmed slightly. "He's not the same kid I used to know."

"Nope. He's a man now. And a pretty damn good-looking one at that," Jess added with a wink.

"Stop." Amy laughed, but her heart wasn't exactly disagreeing with Jess. She'd always had a soft spot for Dante. He was the only thing that ever felt right about this town, the only person who made her second-guess leaving in the first place.

"He's still single, you know," Jess added with a wink.

"I'm not looking for anything," Amy said quickly, though the way her voice wavered made her feel like she was lying. She wasn't ready. Not after Ryan. Not after everything.

But as she glanced out the window again, the mist swirling as the sun began to break through the morning fog, she wondered if maybe—just maybe—coming back to Hidden Creek wasn't about hiding from her past.

Maybe it was about facing it.

In the next few days, as the summer came to an official close, she moved her meager things into the small rental and went back to work at the only job she'd held in the time that she'd lived in Hidden Creek.

Working at Hidden Creek Wine & Liquor had its benefits. For one, now that her brother owned it instead of her uncle, her hours were pretty much whatever she wanted. When her uncle had run the place, she'd been underage and had only been allowed to sweep floors and do the bookkeeping, something she'd been good at from a young age.

While she settled into what would be her new life, Amy found herself getting into a rhythm—something she hadn't felt in years. Her quiet cabin, nestled just outside town, became her sanctuary. At night, she'd sit on the small porch with a glass of wine, the sound of the creek running nearby and the occasional hoot of an owl as her only companions.

Working at the liquor store was a familiar comfort. The regulars, the local gossip, and even the predictability of stocking shelves or ringing up customers felt like slipping back into a well-worn pair of shoes. She appreciated the freedom her brother gave her, though she sometimes wondered if he was too lenient. He never pressed her about the past and never asked why she had come back, which was a relief. Maybe he knew better than anyone that the last thing Amy needed was more questions.

As the longer summer days slowly melted into the shorter, cooler autumn days, she kept busy, her hands and mind always moving, always working, like the constant hum of the creek that ran past her cabin. But no matter how occupied she stayed, there was something—or rather, someone—that kept creeping into her thoughts.

Dante.

She hadn't seen him since that morning at the Coffee Corner. Every time she drove into town, she half-expected to run into him again, but each time, the streets were quiet.

Part of her was relieved. Another part, the part she didn't like to admit, found it disappointing.

"You know, you could always stop by the station," Joe teased her one afternoon while she was stocking a new shipment of wine. "He's not exactly hiding."

"I have no idea who you're talking about," she said dryly.

Joe made a tsking noise. "Everyone in town knows who I'm talking about," he retorted.

Amy scowled and tossed a bottle of merlot into the cooler with more force than necessary. "I'm not avoiding him."

"Sure," Joe said, stretching the word out with a grin. "That's why every time his name comes up, you either go silent or change the subject."

Amy turned her back on him, focusing on arranging the bottles. "I'm just not looking for anything complicated. Last time I was with someone, it was a disaster."

"Yeah, but Dante's not Ryan." Joe's voice softened as he leaned against the counter. "You know that, right?"

She bit her lip. She did know. Dante was the opposite of Ryan in every way that mattered. Where Ryan had been reckless, Dante was steady. Ryan had been volatile, and Dante was patient. But that didn't change the fact that getting close to someone—anyone—felt like stepping too close to the edge of a cliff. One wrong move, and she'd fall over again.

Joe sighed, sensing her hesitation. "Look, all I'm saying is, maybe it's time you stopped running."

Amy froze, his words cutting deeper than she'd like to admit. She wanted to tell him he was wrong, that she wasn't running anymore, that coming back to Hidden Creek had been her way of facing things. But deep down, she knew

The Stars

that even though her feet had stopped, her heart was still in full retreat.

She'd been avoiding her feelings for him since that first kiss, letting fear and overwhelming desire push her toward reckless choices. No wonder she'd always fallen for the wrong guys—she'd never believed in a real future. Before she could come up with a response, the bell over the door chimed, and a customer walked in, saving her from the conversation. Joe shot her a knowing look before turning to greet the man, leaving Amy alone with her thoughts once again.

That evening, after she closed up the shop and made her way back to the cabin, the familiar tension settled in her chest. She parked her car, grabbed her bag, and walked towards the front door, the cool autumn air biting at her skin. The night felt quieter than usual—too quiet. The kind of quiet that makes you hyperaware of every rustle, every shift of the wind.

She shook off the feeling and unlocked the door. Inside, she turned on the lights and tossed her bag on the couch. She poured herself a glass of wine and stepped outside onto the porch. The night sky was clear, the stars visible against the backdrop of inky blackness. She took a long sip, her gaze drifting to the creek that wound its way through the woods.

Her phone buzzed in her pocket, and she glanced at the screen. A message from Jess.

"Having an impromptu get-together tonight around eight. Care to join us at Xtina and Michael's place?"

Amy hesitated, her thumb hovering over the screen. It would be a good distraction. Better than just sitting home alone for another night. And since Jacob and Dante were best friends, if he happened to show up... well, maybe that wouldn't be the worst thing in the world.

Before she could second-guess herself, she typed out a quick response.

"Sounds fun. See you there."

Amy showered and then changed her outfit more than a dozen times in the next hour. She'd avoided clothes shopping since returning home and most of what she had she'd worn in high school. Thankfully, she was the same size as she'd been back then and, even though dated, her clothes still fit perfectly.

Amy stood in front of the mirror, examining her latest outfit: a simple black sweater, a pair of dark jeans, and her old, well-worn boots. She sighed and tugged at the hem of the sweater, wishing she'd gone shopping when she got back into town. High school clothes weren't exactly fashion-forward, and she hadn't been great at fashion even back then. Still, it was comfortable enough, and she wasn't trying to make a grand entrance. She was just showing up for a casual evening with friends... and possibly running into Dante.

Her heart gave an annoying little jump at the thought of him, but she shoved it down. It wasn't like anything was going to happen. She hadn't seen him since that morning at the Coffee Corner, and chances were, tonight wouldn't be any different.

She grabbed her jacket and headed out the door, locking up the cabin behind her. The night air was crisp. Fall was officially in full swing. The drive to Xtina and Michael's place was short. The road wound through the woods as her headlights cast long shadows across the tall trees overhead.

Spooky season, she thought as she drove.

When she pulled up to the house, she could already hear the low hum of laughter and music spilling out from the backyard.

The Stars

Xtina had always lived in one of the oldest buildings in or around town. She'd inherited the home a while back when her parents had died in a car accident, which later on had been determined to be murder. A cult leader had caused her parents' deaths and then stalked Xtina and kidnapped her.

The home was a massive plantation style two-story house that sat just outside town. It was surrounded by massive, ancient oak trees. The property had a huge sprawling yard that made it perfect for get-togethers like this.

Amy took a deep breath, trying to settle the nerves that had been bubbling up inside her since she'd agreed to come over. She wasn't usually this anxious about social events, but returning to Hidden Creek had stirred up so many old feelings—nostalgia, regret, and hope all wrapped up into one confusing knot. She wasn't sure how to untangle it.

"Just a few hours. You can handle a few hours," she whispered to herself before heading around the side of the house to the backyard.

"I see you still talk to yourself," a deep voice said from behind her. She squealed and spun around. Dante's smile flashed as he moved closer to her, seemingly sliding out of the darkness.

His skin glowed in the soft light from the overhead fairy lights that hung in the large oak trees that surrounded the parking area of the property.

His dark eyes ran over her, heating her until she desperately wished she could pull off her jacket.

"I see you still enjoy sneaking up on people," she replied, causing him to chuckle.

She felt foolish, so she didn't wait for his response but

turned on her heels and headed towards the noise, knowing full well that he'd fall in step with her.

They remained quiet as they walked down the side pathway around the massive house.

As soon as they rounded the corner, she spotted Jess sitting on a lounge chair, laughing at something Michael had just said.

Xtina was playing with a dog as she drank a beer, her dark hair pulled back into a high ponytail. There had been many rumors about the woman floating around town in the past few years, but that was nothing compared to the rumors the kids had spread about her growing up. Still, Amy had never had a reason to dislike Xtina. Actually, she'd always admired her for her strength in friendship. Xtina and Jess had been best friends for as long as anyone could remember. Through thick or thin, the two women stuck together.

Amy had shared a few friendships with a handful of people in her past, none of whom she was still connected to.

Jess and Xtina had always been best friends. Amy could tell that the duo was even closer now than before.

Joe and Liz were there, quietly talking in a swing closer to the back of the home. Her brother nodded and waved at her when he spotted her. Liz looked slightly uncomfortable with her heavy pregnancy but smiled at her when she waved.

Michael's brother Ethan, whom she'd met a few times before, now was married to Brea, a petite blonde woman who kept looking at her funny.

Tara and Selene were sisters but looked nothing alike, but she could see the resemblance between Selene and Lucas.

She was thankful that Lucas and Mia were there and

The Stars

enjoyed catching up with the couple. Most everyone here occasionally came into the liquor store, but this was the first time she was socializing with any of them outside of that first day she'd returned to town.

"Amy! You made it!" Jess waved her over, a wide grin on her face. "Dante's here too." She laughed.

Amy smiled and waved back, the knot in her chest loosening just a little. "Yeah, we bumped into one another out front."

"Come sit with us," Jess said, patting the chair next to her.

She moved over and sat down just as Dante took the chair next to Jacob and started chatting with him.

Her heart skipped a beat as he leaned back in one of the Adirondack chairs, opened a beer, and took a sip while his eyes locked with hers.

Shadows from the firelight played over his dark skin, highlighting his facial features and making his sharp jawline look even more defined. He already looked relaxed, laughing at something Jacob had said, and for a moment, Amy just sat there, frozen. Totally enamored by him.

The feelings he brought out in her, the things that just his simple glances did to her, well, she thought about running, making any excuse to leave. Jess reached over and touched her arm, pulling her out of her thoughts. "I can see it in your eyes. I'm not going to let you escape this quickly. You just got here."

Reluctantly, Amy relaxed in the lounge chair, doing her best to keep her eyes from straying back to Dante. But it was no use. She could feel his presence like a gravitational pull and couldn't stop glancing over at him again. It didn't help that every time she looked, he seemed to catch her eye, too, his gaze lingering just a second too long.

Almost an hour after she'd arrived, Mia stood up and got everyone's attention.

"Tonight. It's tonight," she said suddenly, her eyes going around the group quickly and then landing on her for a brief second before asking the group. "Is everyone ready?"

Amy frowned as everyone around her suddenly sobered and nodded before turning to look directly at her and Dante.

"What?" she asked after a moment of silence.

"Tonight is the night that you will finally fulfill your destiny," Mia said firmly with a grin.

Chapter Four

Dante didn't know what to expect from the evening. He'd hung around Jacob and the group of his friends many times over the past few years. At first, he hadn't been the only single player but in the past few months, everyone had paired up. He supposed that was why Amy had been invited, along with being Joe's little sister.

While everyone sat around the firepit chatting and having fun, he watched Amy closely. She seemed nervous at first and then settled into conversation with a few others. While he tried not to eavesdrop, he couldn't help but overhear a little of the conversation.

"So, how's it been, settling back into town?" he overheard Jess asking Amy shortly after they had arrived.

"It's... it's been good," Amy answered. He noticed the pause and glanced her way and caught her eyes moving over towards him. "Quiet, mostly. I'm still getting used to being back in town."

Jess nodded. "It'll feel normal again soon. Trust me. You've rented the Meyers cabin, right?"

"Yes." Amy's sigh was that of pleasure. "I've always loved it up there. We used to go fishing and camping there every summer. Now that Carl Meyers has passed, Larry, his son, is renting the place out. Normally he rents the place out on Airbnb, but he's thrilled that I've signed a six-month lease."

"Didn't think you'd be here tonight." Michael slapped him on the shoulder, getting his attention.

"Joe insisted." He shrugged and glanced towards Amy's brother and sister-in-law.

"You two were best friends in school, right?" Michael sat next to him.

"Yup. We started off playing little league together."

He heard Amy laugh and glanced over in her direction.

As the evening continued, he didn't get a chance to chat with her directly until he went inside to grab another drink while she was getting one for herself.

"So, I guess you finally made the list to get into this exclusive party," he joked.

She leaned against the countertop and opened her beer before she responded.

"I guess. I didn't know this was the hot spot in town," she said with a smile.

"Oh, it's a real elite place. High class." He glanced at her worn boots. "But you fit in perfectly."

She laughed. "It must be high class if you're here."

Dante chuckled. "You make it sound like seeing me is a bad thing."

Amy bit her lip, and suddenly he was very aware of how close he was to her, of how his arm brushed hers when he moved. "I didn't say that."

He didn't reply right away, but his smile lingered, the silence between them thick with things unsaid. Before the tension could grow any thicker, Xtina came inside to get some more wine and interrupted them.

The rest of the night passed in a blur of laughter and stolen glances.

Shortly before midnight, the atmosphere suddenly changed when Mia stood up and announced, "Tonight. It's tonight. Is everyone ready?"

"What?" Amy asked after a moment of silence.

"Tonight is the night that you will finally fulfill your destiny," Mia said firmly with a grin.

Everyone turned to one another and began whispering, and then Jacob stood up and suggested they all go for a walk.

The group began to move, everyone somehow persuading Amy and Dante to follow them across the field. Dante's mind was still spinning as they walked towards the old Anderson farm—the place he'd spent the last few years chasing kids out of. He knew all too well that the underground silo loomed ahead of them. Its massive underground maze, stretched out like spider webs beneath their feet, had been a death trap for some.

The place had a reputation—a bad one. This was the very place where Xtina had been kidnapped by the cult leader. The same place where more than one person had lost their life.

They had just reached the middle of the field when Mia stopped and turned to him. "I'm sorry, really, about what's going to happen to you. Just know that, in the end, things will be set right."

Dante's mind raced as he tried to piece together what Mia was saying.

The entire group had been acting strange all night, their behavior growing more cryptic by the second. But when

Mia spoke, the look in her eyes was different—serious, almost desperate.

Mia's gaze flickered between him and Amy before she spoke again, her voice soft but carrying an undeniable weight.

"What we're doing here, right now, is because the fate of all worlds depends on it. Everything. Every timeline, every reality—it hinges on what the two of you do next. Where you go from here."

Dante blinked, trying to comprehend the enormity of her words. "The fate of all worlds?" he echoed, disbelief lacing his voice. "This is a joke, right?"

It sounded like something out of a sci-fi movie, something far removed from the reality he'd always known. He wanted to laugh at the group's joke. Surely they were being punked.

However, Mia's expression was unwavering. "There are forces at play that you can't see, can't understand fully yet. But trust me, what's about to happen was fated long before any of us were born. Long before Hidden Creek even existed."

Amy stepped forward, her arms wrapped tightly around herself, her brow furrowed in confusion. "What are you talking about? How could we have anything to do with the fate of... worlds? This is crazy!"

Mia's expression softened slightly as she turned to Amy. "It might sound crazy, I know. But it's the truth. Everything that has happened in your lives, every strange event, every inexplicable moment—it's all led to this. You and Dante are at the center of something much bigger than just Hidden Creek, much bigger than anything you've ever imagined."

Dante could feel his pulse pounding in his ears. "What

The Stars

do you mean?" His mind was spinning. Fate? Worlds? What the hell had he gotten dragged into?

Mia exhaled slowly as if searching for the right words. "The two of you... You've been chosen. This has all been written in the threads of time. Everything we do, every decision, ripples across dimensions, across worlds. And right now, those threads are unraveling. The fabric of time itself is fraying. But you and Amy—you're the ones who can stop it. That's why we're here. That's why you're here."

"Okay, you've had your fun." He reached for Amy's hand to pull her back towards the house.

"I am a djinn," Mia said loudly. He and Amy glanced back and watched in shock as the small Asian woman shifted. Her size grew by a hundred percent and she glowed, growing, until the entire mass blocked out the moonlight.

"Is... that a dragon?" Amy gasped.

"I am Helios," Lucas said, and he shifted into a massive black dog, half the size of the dragon.

"I am Hecate," Jess said. She lifted off the ground surrounded by a circle of green and blue mist. Then she shot lightning between her fingertips.

"We are sisters Tara and Selene, daughters of goddess Rhea and god Typhon." The two sisters also lifted off the ground and hovered almost a hundred feet off the ground.

Dante and Amy stood in the field, gaping at the group of friends.

"How... what are we supposed to do?" she asked, her voice barely above a whisper.

Just as quickly as everyone morphed or flew, they were all back on the ground as themselves again.

He'd known some of these people for years, some of them his entire life. How long had they had these powers?

"What about the rest of you?" he asked, locking eyes with Jacob and Joe.

"Some of us have hidden powers." Jacob shrugged.

"Some of us have less... showy powers," Joe said, his eyes locking with Amy's.

"Are you saying we have powers?" Amy asked.

Mia stepped closer to them, then hesitated for a moment. She shook her head. "I can't tell you that. All I know is what's going to happen has to happen naturally. You just need to trust us and trust yourselves."

Dante's stomach twisted with a mix of fear and frustration. "So you're saying everything depends on us? And you can't even tell us what we're supposed to do?"

Mia gave him a look filled with sympathy and something that looked suspiciously like guilt. "It's not that simple. If I tell you too much, it could change things. We can't risk that. All I can say is that we—" she gestured to the group standing around them—"we stand for the greater good. There is a threat coming that wants to destroy everything. For us to have a chance to fight, you must both take a journey. You'll understand in time."

Before Dante could press her further, Mia turned to the group and spoke the strangest words he had ever heard.

"Our presence here is not a coincidence," Mia said, her voice laced with a quiet certainty. "We are all more than we realize, more than anyone knows. Our bloodline... our very existence is tied to this moment, to everything that's about to happen." She turned towards him. "You are the key to unlocking Amy's past, her future, and her powers." Her eyes locked with his.

Amy's breath hitched audibly. "What are you talking about? My powers? I'm just... me."

Mia's gaze softened with what looked like compassion.

The Stars

"You're more than you know, Amy. Far more. The power that runs through your veins... it's ancient, tied to forces long forgotten. And now, it's time for you to realize that. It's time for you to awaken."

Amy took a step back, shaking her head. "No. No, this doesn't make any sense. I'm not... I'm not some chosen one or whatever you think I am."

Dante wanted to step in, to shield Amy from this overwhelming, bizarre reality, but he found himself frozen, trying to process it all.

They had just witnessed Mia turn into a dragon and Lucas into a giant dog. A few others had flown.

He had so many questions. What was Mia talking about? Powers? Bloodlines? And how the hell were they both connected to something this big? Every single person standing in the circle seemed to be insane. Even Jacob was in on it. Were they all crazy?

Maybe they'd been drugged? That was it. All sorts of things could cause them to hallucinate.

He knew about some of the past events that the group had gone through. How Jess had been dubbed a witch. The rumors of Xtina's powers. They had just been rumors. Right?

Before he could voice any of his concerns, Jacob stepped forward, his face grim. "It's time," he said, his voice low and resolute. "We need to head down now."

The group moved quickly through the opened door, down the main entrance of the silo. As they walked, Jess flicked her wrist, and overhead lights turned on as if by magic.

"What's going on?" Amy whispered to him.

He reached out for her hand in the dim light and held

on as they made their way through the maze, finally stepping into the main silo room.

"Jess?" Mia asked.

Suddenly, there was a loud noise as the heavy metal door of the silo lifted and opened.

Amy wrapped her arms tighter around herself, clearly unnerved. "Is this really happening?" she asked, her voice shaking.

Dante wanted to comfort her, to tell her everything would be fine, but he didn't have those answers. He didn't even know what was happening himself. And then, as if on cue, the clouds overhead parted, revealing the full moon in all its silvery glory high overhead. The moonlight poured into the silo, flooding over them like a spotlight, casting long, eerie shadows over the group.

There was a sudden shift in the air, a change in tension around them. He felt a cold, unnerving certainty that whatever was coming next was inevitable. That fate, ancient and unstoppable, was finally closing in.

Dante barely had time to process what was going on before Brea stepped forward and touched his shoulder. Her fingers were cool and delicate, but the moment they made contact, a shock ran through him like lightning striking deep into his bones.

"She will have to go forward first," Brea told him, her voice laced with mystery. "You'll meet her in the past. This is how it has to be."

Dante opened his mouth to argue, to demand an explanation, but before a single word could escape his lips, everything shifted. A burning, electric sensation exploded in his chest, racing through every nerve in his body. It wasn't pain —not exactly—but it was overwhelming, like being hit with an unrelenting surge of energy. His skin tingled, his muscles clenched involuntarily, and his heart pounded as if it might burst from his chest with an unknown force.

He gasped, trying to ground himself, but it was like touching a live wire. The buzzing in his ears grew louder, vibrating in the very core of his skull until he could hear nothing else. It was as if the world itself was humming, tearing apart at the seams. Bright, searing light flooded his vision, forcing his eyes shut, but even then, the light seemed to burn through his eyelids.

The world beneath his feet began to spin violently, faster and faster. His stomach lurched, as though he were on the edge of a cliff, teetering in that brief, terrifying moment before the fall. But then the ground vanished completely, leaving him suspended in nothingness.

He was falling.

Free-falling.

Dante's arms flailed as he screamed, reaching for something—anything—to grab onto, to stop his plunge into the unknown void. The wind roared in his ears, or was it the buzzing still? He wasn't sure anymore. Everything was a chaotic blur, his senses overwhelmed by the sheer impossibility of what was happening. His chest tightened with panic as the sensation of falling deepened. His heart was hammering so fast that it felt like it might give out at any moment. There was neither up nor down—just a dizzying vortex of motion and light.

And then, as suddenly as it began, it stopped.

He landed, but not on jagged rocks or an unforgiving surface. The impact was soft and yielding. Warm. His breath came in ragged gasps as the world righted itself, the spinning sensation easing enough for him to dare open his eyes.

Sand.

Golden grains clung to his hands, to his skin, shifting through his fingers as he pushed himself up. He was still reeling from the sensation of being hurled through space when he took a deep breath. The sand was warm beneath him, heated by a sun far brighter and more intense than the one from the world he'd known just moments ago.

He sat there for a moment, catching his breath, his heart still pounding hard in his chest as he tried to make sense of where he was—or when he was. The air around him was salty and heavy, and the sound of waves crashed softly feet from him.

Wherever he was, the beach stretched out before him for miles. The clear water sparkled under the bright midday sun, stretching endlessly towards the horizon. The coastline was rugged and wild, with jagged cliffs rising in the distance, their peaks softened by the haze of heat shimmering off the ocean. Behind him, a dense forest of olive trees and tall, swaying grasses rustled in the warm breeze. The air was alive with the faint hum of insects.

Dante's fingers curled into the sand, grounding him. He could still feel the lingering hum of energy coursing through his veins, like static clinging to his skin, but it was fading, the remnants of Brea's power slowly dissipating.

He swallowed hard, his throat dry as he tried to process what had just happened. The soft roar of the ocean waves was calming, yet surreal. This wasn't a beach he recognized —he wasn't anywhere near Hidden Creek, or anywhere he had ever been. The sky above him was clear, the kind of deep, perfect blue that seemed to stretch on forever. He blinked, squinting against the brightness, still struggling to piece together how he had gone from the grip of Brea's magic to landing here.

The realization hit him like a punch to the gut, stealing

The Stars

the breath he'd only just regained. He was here. Really here. This wasn't a dream. He hadn't been drugged. Everything he'd just witnessed was real.

Dante pushed himself to his feet, his legs shaky, the sand shifting under his shoes. The weight of the moment settled on his shoulders like a heavy cloak, his mind racing with questions. What was he supposed to do now?

He turned in a slow circle, scanning the beach, the distant cliffs, and the endless sea. Everything felt impossibly different, untouched by time, like stepping into a long-forgotten myth. The air smelled of salt, the breeze carrying the distant cry of seabirds. He felt impossibly small, standing on the edge of a different world.

A deep breath of the warm, salty air filled his lungs as he began to walk along the shoreline, the sand shifting beneath his boots with each step. The distant cliffs loomed ahead and, beyond them, who knew what waited?

As he walked, his pulse finally began to slow, the panic receding. But there was no denying it—he was far from anything familiar. And he had a long road ahead of him in this strange world.

Chapter Five

Amy hadn't realized she'd been the one to scream as Dante disappeared before her eyes.

This had to be a trick. Right?

Her friends and brother were somehow playing a huge joke on them. Dante must be in on it. That's it. That makes sense.

But then she replayed what she'd just witnessed.

Dante's entire body had... shimmered and vanished when Brea had touched his shoulder.

Now, Brea was moving towards her.

"No!" She held up her hands. "I..." She looked towards her brother. Joe was nodding at her and had a strange smile on his lips. Then he mouthed, "Trust us."

She shook her head. "This isn't right."

Before Brea could touch her, Mia stepped forward.

"Remember who you are," she said. "It's time to wake up, Pandora." She lightly touched her fingertips to Amy's temples. Her entire world spun quickly and an odd warmth spread through her.

Memories flashed before her eyes, too quickly for any of the scenes to make sense.

Mia stood in a great hall under a dark sky filled with three moons. There were huge, intricate glass chandeliers hanging from large beams that crossed high overhead.

Before her was a single large golden chair on a pedestal. Two suns were setting directly behind the throne.

Amy was slightly shocked to see herself and Hope, Dante's sister, standing at the head of the room.

Hope was dressed in a long flowing silver and lavender gown and her dark skin practically glowed, as if it had been sprayed with tiny golden sparkles. A large sleek silver crown sat on top of her jet-black hair.

Amy was dressed in a flowing golden gown. Her paler skin appeared as if it were made of stardust, and her long golden hair held a crown of gold that gleamed brightly in the dying sunlight.

Then Hope moved forward and lifted her arms.

"Welcome, Mia Li, daughter of Malik al-Ahmar," Hope said clearly. "We are sorry for keeping you waiting so long for answers. We needed to be assured of a few things and had to get everything in order for our departure."

"We have been expecting you for a very long time," Amy added.

"I am Elpis," Hope said with a slight smile. "This is my sister Pandora." Hope turned towards Amy, who smiled in return.

Then, just as quickly as the images appeared, they were gone. Brea's hands replaced Mia's on her face, and Amy blinked a few times to focus on the other woman's silver eyes.

The world around Amy felt like it was collapsing, unraveling thread by thread. Brea's voice echoed in her head, distant and haunting, the words taking on a weight that pressed against her chest.

"You must go forward to wake and see the possibilities," Brea had said, her voice trembling with emotion as if burdened by a truth too heavy to bear. A tear slipped down her cheek, catching the faint glimmer of moonlight. "When you see him again, everything will be revealed. This is what we know. This is all we can tell you. You are the next step in saving this world."

Amy's mind reeled at the words—saving the world? How could that possibly be true? She was just... her. Ordinary, flawed, and lost in a storm that she didn't understand. But before she could protest, before she could demand answers, she felt the strangest sensation. Brea's touch seared into her skin, sending an electric pulse deep into her core. The spots where Brea had made contact began to burn, then tingle, a quick zap of electricity rushing from those points into her very bones.

It spread fast—hot, sharp, invasive—like a live wire snaking through her insides. She gasped, her body jerking involuntarily as the electric charge consumed her, ripping through muscle and tissue, a force so violent that she felt like her very atoms were being torn apart. A scream ripped from her throat, but the sound was swallowed by the air around her. It echoed only in her own mind, a chilling, hollow scream that went unanswered.

Her vision blurred as everything began to spin, the world around her becoming a kaleidoscope of lights and shadows. Her body felt weightless, as though it was unraveling, disintegrating. Her heart raced, panic setting in with a ferocity she had never experienced before.

Why? Why was this happening?

Her thoughts clashed together, wild and frantic. *Is this*

what happened to Dante? she wondered, the thought slicing through the chaos. *Is this what he felt?*

Then, as quickly as it had begun, it all stopped. The spinning, the electricity, the sensation of being torn apart—it all vanished. The world fell silent.

Amy stood still, gasping for breath, her heart hammering in her chest. Slowly, cautiously, she opened her eyes. The darkness around her was thick and unnerving, an oppressive void that swallowed everything. She was in the same spot in the Anderson field above the silo as before—or so it seemed—but now, she was alone.

The clouds had blocked out the stars and moonlight, causing her to second-guess everything.

Confusion twisted her stomach into knots. She turned in slow, bewildered circles, calling out desperately. "Joe? This isn't funny," she yelled, her voice trembling with a mix of fear and anger. "Come on, where are you?"

But there was no answer. No laughter, no teasing voices from her friends hiding in the grass. The silence pressed in on her, thick and eerie, settling over her like a suffocating blanket.

Realizing her friends weren't there, Amy began walking back across the darkened field, the cold prickle of unease growing stronger with every step. The tall grass tugged at her legs, and she kept stumbling, her feet catching on unseen roots and rocks. The clouds blocked what little moonlight there was, barely illuminating her path.

"How did I ever think this was fun?" she muttered bitterly to herself, remembering the reckless nights she'd spent sneaking out here with friends in high school. Back then, the silo had been a playground for their drunken antics, a place to get high and let go. Now, it felt like a graveyard.

Her frustration morphed into outright anger. What kind of sick joke was this? How had they done it? She couldn't wrap her head around what had happened, the bizarre sensation of being torn apart, the disappearance of everyone she knew. Not to mention the dragon, the dog, and the flying.

As she approached the place where Michael and Xtina's house should have been, her steps faltered. She stopped dead in her tracks.

Where the massive house once stood, there was... nothing. No house, no lights, no familiar structure. Just an empty, gaping hole where the home had once been.

Amy blinked, her legs suddenly weak beneath her. Her knees buckled, and she slid to the ground, staring in disbelief. "No... no, this can't be right," she whispered, her voice cracking. Panic surged up, hot and fast, clawing at her chest. "Joe! Anyone!" she screamed, her voice breaking into huge, heaving sobs.

The night remained silent.

Her breath came in short gasps as she looked around, trying to make sense of it. The air was warmer, unnervingly so. It had been a cool, crisp night—she remembered the breeze biting at her skin—but now it felt... wrong. Warm. Hot, even.

Then an odd light shone down on her.

Was that the sun coming up already?

She glanced towards the horizon, expecting to see the early rays of dawn creeping in, but something was off. The warmth, the stillness in the air, the unsettling quiet. It all felt... unnatural. Like the world itself was holding its breath.

Amy stumbled to her feet, her legs shaky as she continued forward, leaving the empty void where the house had once stood. She moved towards the tree line, the woods that had always been a comforting, familiar presence. But as she stepped into the clearing, something stopped her cold.

There, in the night sky, hung the moon. Or what was left of it. Large, shattered pieces of the celestial body floated in the sky, fractured and broken like a ruined puzzle, suspended in a vast and empty void of space thousands of miles above the earth.

Amy stared, wide-eyed, her heart pounding in her ears. The shattered moon cast an eerie glow over the landscape, a haunting reminder that wherever she was, it wasn't the place she'd known. This wasn't her world.

She wasn't where she belonged.

Her throat tightened as a single thought cut through the haze of her shock. What the hell had happened?

It took her a few minutes to decide what to do. With her heart pounding in her chest, she stumbled down the road leading to Hidden Creek. The town, once filled with the hum of life, was eerily silent. Her legs ached from the long walk, but she pushed forward, the unsettling quiet around her pushing her faster. She didn't know what had happened, but something was deeply wrong. The image of the shattered moon hung in her mind like a nightmare she couldn't shake. Even when the clouds covered the destruction again, she could still see it in her mind.

The town came into view, but it too was far from the place she remembered. The usually bustling streets were empty, and buildings stood dark and abandoned or destroyed. Every single window was broken, the sidewalks cracked, cars overturned or burned beyond recognition. A thick layer of dust covered everything.

As she neared what used to be the town center, she saw movement—a shadow darting behind a building. Her breath caught. She paused, unsure if it was friend or foe.

The Stars

"Amy!" a hushed voice called from the other side. She whipped her head around and spotted Jess peeking out from behind a rusty pickup truck parked near the old diner.

"Jess!" Amy ran towards her, relief flooding her chest. As she neared, she saw more familiar faces hiding in the shadows—Jacob, Michael, Xtina, and a few others from the town. They all looked older, and worn, like they had been through hell.

Before she could ask a single question, Jess grabbed her arm and pulled her towards the truck.

"We don't have time. We need to move. Now!" Jess's voice was tight with urgency. "He's crossing the road."

Just then she glanced over her shoulder and saw a dark shadow slink across the road. It was roughly the size of a bear yet it had no fur.

"Run," Jess said, and Amy was pulled quickly towards another truck. She was shoved in alongside Jess.

"What the hell is going on?" Amy demanded, but the others were already piling into the truck.

The truck rumbled to life, and Jacob hit the gas, speeding them out of town and towards the outskirts, heading back in the direction she'd just come from. Back towards the silo.

"Amy." A voice caught her attention from the front seat. She turned, locking eyes with her brother. He looked different—older, harder, his face drawn with exhaustion.

"Joe? What—?" She shook her head as she took in everything about him. He was skinnier. Gone were the massive muscles he'd had most of his adult life. Instead, he looked like a man who had starved. He was still strong, yes, but instead of the lovable meathead he'd always been, he was lean, toned, and... tired.

He cut her off. "I know it's hard to wrap your mind

around, but it's ten years since I last saw you. The last time we saw you was in the silo, right?"

She nodded quickly. "I... ended up in the field," she said stupidly.

"That night, ten years ago, Brea sent you here. We've been expecting you, sometime soon. We just didn't know the exact date and time or place." He shook his head.

Her breath caught in her throat. Ten years?

"Everything's changed," Joe continued, his voice grave. "More than half the population on earth is dead. When they attacked, that first night, they shattered the moon, and well, everything fell apart after that." He shrugged and glanced out the window quickly.

She glanced back and watched as the dark figure chased after them.

"We have to lose him before we go back," Jacob said. "Everyone hang on."

"They're fast but stupid," Joe explained.

"Who? What?" She shook her head but then held in a scream as Jacob turned the truck quickly down a back alley.

"Harpies," Jess answered as they held on. "They've been working with the other gods."

Amy's stomach twisted with dread. "Gods? Who? Who attacked?" Were they in danger now? What were Harpies? Were they chasing them? She glanced behind them and could still only see darkness.

No one answered her as Jacob weaved through what remained of the town.

"We're clear," Jess said, closing her eyes.

The truck slowed and took the turn that would lead them back out of town.

Amy wanted to scream, to demand more answers, but there was something in the silence of the truck that made

The Stars

her stay quiet. Instead, she gripped the seat tightly as her mind raced to keep up with the whirlwind of information.

"What about everyone? The town? Our family?" she asked, her voice barely a whisper.

Joe's expression darkened, and for a moment, he didn't answer. Then, with a sigh that seemed to carry the weight of the world, he said, "Liz didn't make it. She died during the first wave of attacks."

Amy's chest constricted. "Liz? No..." She felt her body tense.

"But the triplets survived," Joe added quickly. "Luna, Stella, and Orion. They're with us. They've been with us since... since everything went to hell."

Amy swallowed hard, trying to process it all. Her sister-in-law was gone, but her nieces and nephew had survived. Triplets? Shit. Liz had been pregnant with triplets. They hadn't told anyone there were three of them. Had it been a secret they'd hoped to surprise everyone with?

Joe continued, "We've been hiding out at the silo. It's the only safe place. It's become a fortress we have to protect twenty-four-seven. There's a whole group of us now, nearly a hundred people. We've made it our home. It's not much, but it's safe. For now. We are the protectors. We do what we can using what we have." He glanced over at Jacob. "We're stronger together. They can't break through that."

The truck sped along the abandoned roads, the dark landscape blurring past them. The closer they got to the silo, the more her fear gnawed at her. What had happened to the world? Who had done this? Gods? What gods?

As they pulled up to the cave entrance of the silo, Amy saw that the thick rock walls were now fortified. There were guards stationed all around it with several on the hillside.

They were all dressed in full camo and scanned the surroundings with scoped guns and night-vision goggles.

She'd always gone into the silo using the old doorway in the field, taking the staircase down into the heart of it. She'd never really known of the cave entrance until someone told her about it a few years back. She knew it was easier to get lost using the long narrow tunnels when going in this way.

They were let in without a word, and the truck rumbled down into the underground complex, stopping a few feet into a large low-lit tunnel.

Once they were inside, Joe helped her out of the truck and hugged her, holding on for a long moment before stepping back. He felt so different. Smelled different too. Musty. Sweaty. Raw.

Gone was her goofy meathead brother. He'd been replaced by a frail man who had lost... everything.

From there, they walked in silence through the dimly lit tunnels that narrowed as they wound further into the massive complex.

When they finally stepped into the large silo area, Amy looked around, her eyes wide as she took in the sight.

The silo had been transformed into an underground refuge. It was like a small hidden city. People moved about, cooking, working, trying to survive. Makeshift homes lined the walls, and boxes and crates of supplies were stacked neatly in corners. There was a strange sense of calm, but also of constant vigilance, like everyone was waiting for the next disaster to strike.

As they made their way through the compound, someone came running towards them—Brea. She looked frantic, her eyes wide with guilt and relief as she reached her.

"Amy!" Brea threw her arms around her, pulling her

The Stars

into a tight embrace. "I'm so sorry. I'm so sorry for sending you here."

Amy pulled back, confused. "I... don't understand."

Brea nodded, tears welling up in her eyes. "It was the only way... to save all of us. I didn't want you to see this place, this possible future. But in order for it to change, I had no choice."

"Save us from this?" Amy asked, confused. "How?"

Brea took a deep breath, her expression grim. "You had to see this, in order to save us all from the gods."

Amy blinked several times. Everyone kept saying that. "The gods?"

Brea nodded, her face pale. "The gods destroyed our world. They shattered the moon, decimated our population, and now they use the Harpies to hunt us. We've been hiding here ever since. This place is our only shelter." She glanced around. "We use our powers, the ones you saw that night, to protect it, to hide it from them. At least for now. But... you're the only one who can actually stop all of this from happening in the first place. You're the only one who can save us from this fate."

Amy staggered back, her mind reeling. "Me? How? I don't understand."

"It's your destiny," Mia said softly as she stepped forward. "This was fated long before any of us were born. You and Dante... the two of you are the key to stopping all this from happening." She hugged Amy. When she stepped back, she added. "I showed you my memories that we shared. Remember?"

Amy's blood ran cold as she remembered the vision she'd had when Mia had touched her.

"Pandora must wake," Mia said with a sigh.

"Let me get this right." She felt her chest tighten. She

had been thrown into a future where everything she knew was gone, where half the world was dead, and now she was being told that she was supposed to save them from the wrath of the gods. It was too much. "I... I can't... save everyone."

Mia took her hands, squeezing them tightly. "You can. You have to. Our entire future depends on it."

Chapter Six

Dante trudged through the foreign landscape. The heat of the sun was relentless, its intensity more searing than anything he'd felt before. He had long since discarded his jacket and had slung it over his shoulders. His shirt had followed not long after. The heat seemed to radiate off everything, so he'd tied it around his head for a little more shade.

He had determined right away to stick to walking on the edge of the water instead of trudging through the thick trees that surrounded the beach. This way he could dip in the cool water when he overheated, which he had a few times already. Each time, he'd removed his clothes until he was walking around in his boxer shorts and shoes.

His feet started to ach with each step, and he figured he'd been walking almost three hours so far. The landscape stretched on for as far as he could see. Directly beside the long stretch of beach was a mixture of rugged terrain and rolling hills. Eventually, the harsh landscape gave way to a stunning valley, which he decided to explore after seeing hints of life. Long fields filled with some sort of crops had been a welcome sight.

As he descended into the valley, he saw a small village nestled at the base of a looming, jagged mountain. The town looked ancient and was made up of low stone buildings with thatched roofs. Dusty, worn paths wound between them. Surrounding the village was a patchwork of fields that stretched out for miles, their crops basking under the shadow of the looming peak.

Mount Olympus, he realized with a slight shock. He recognized it from a few videos and pictures that he'd seen of the area. He'd always dreamed of visiting Greece someday.

If it wasn't for the obviously ancient buildings and the lack of modern machinery, he would have just assumed it was a small untouched modern village.

The village itself seemed eerily quiet at first, save for the distant bleating of goats and the murmur of the wind through the crops. As Dante got closer, he noticed people—simple farmers and townsfolk—going about their daily business. When they spotted him, however, they stopped what they were doing and gathered around him.

A group of them stepped out from stone buildings, their gazes locked onto him as though he were an apparition. The men were dressed in short, loose linen robes and sandals. The women wore similar robes but slightly longer, and some of them carried clay jugs or wooden tools. Children, dressed in shorter versions of the same clothes, gathered around him, reaching out and touching his dark skin with childlike curiosity.

The sun-darkened skin of the men and women spoke of lives spent laboring under the sun. Still, they were more olive toned than his own rich blackness. He wondered if they'd ever seen a Black person before. His serious lack of history lessons frustrated him for the first time in his life.

He remembered a few stories of how Africans had visited the Egyptians before. But this was Greece and he wasn't sure just when he was.

Their reaction to him unsettled him. Thankfully, they didn't appear to be afraid of him. Instead, their reaction was more akin to awe. His heart raced as he continued his steady walk forward, his dark skin and modern jeans anachronistic in the extreme. His footsteps echoed in the quiet as whispers surged through the crowd, rippling like the wind.

"M-Mythos... Epimetheus," someone whispered, their voice trembling with disbelief.

Dante froze when he recognized the name. Epimetheus? That was a figure from Greek mythology, the brother of Prometheus. Did they think that's who he was? But why would they think that?

"Epimetheus!" another voice cried, this one stronger, more certain. "The god has returned!"

Suddenly, the villagers rushed forward, surrounding him like the children had. They fell to their knees in front of him and bowed their heads low, as though they were in the presence of divinity. Dante's mind reeled as they muttered praises in what sounded like ancient Greek. And yet... he could understand them. It was like his mind was translating their words automatically, something that shouldn't be possible.

He swallowed hard, trying to make sense of what was happening. His mouth went dry as he looked at the villagers, their faces shining with hope and reverence. Could this be a part of the spell, or was there something else at work?

"I... I'm not..." he stammered, but his voice was

drowned out by the rising wave of exclamations from the crowd.

"Epimetheus has returned!" an older man shouted. "The gods have answered our prayers!"

"The gods?" Dante repeated, bewildered.

He looked over the heads of the kneeling villagers towards the looming Mount Olympus. Of course. The gods. Greek gods. The myths about deities ruling over humans started around twenty-seven hundred years ago. Which could mean that he had been sent back to somewhere near 700 BCE.

The people continued to chant his supposed name—Epimetheus—their voices rising in feverish devotion. His pulse raced. Whatever they believed, it was tied to something much larger than he could understand at that moment. But one thing was clear: they thought he was their god.

Brea's cryptic words echoed in his mind: *"Everything will be revealed. This is what we know. This is all we can tell you. You are the next step in saving this world."*

"Water," he asked once all the chanting died down, and seconds later a clay cup was thrust into his hands. He drank deeply until his thirst was quenched.

Before he could utter another word, a man in his early fifties approached. Unlike the others, this man didn't kneel or tremble. Instead, he regarded Dante with a discerning eye, his weathered face framed by a beard streaked with silver. His clothes were finer than those of the villagers, his tunic intricately embroidered, and around his neck hung a medallion that marked him as someone of importance.

"You must come with me," the man said, his voice firm yet respectful. "Please, I am the village leader. I have been directed to help you, Epimetheus."

The Stars

Dante hesitated but realized he had no choice. The people believed he was something divine, and if he was to learn anything about why he was here—or how he could possibly return—he needed to play along, at least for now.

The man led him through the narrow streets and welcomed him to Thessalia, which Dante instantly realized was the name of the town. They moved past humble homes built of stone and timber as the children and some of the townspeople followed along.

Once they stepped outside of town, however, everyone else dropped back. As they climbed higher into the valley, Dante's gaze drifted to the imposing presence of Mount Olympus, its peaks shrouded in mist as the evening began to set in. The air grew cooler as they approached a large structure perched atop a hill. It wasn't a grand temple like the ones in his history books, but more of a sacred gathering place—a sanctuary of sorts, built from smooth marble and adorned with carvings of gods and goddesses.

He briefly wondered if this place was still standing in the future. He'd never heard of a town called Thessalia, but he knew there were plenty such villages near the base of Olympus that had been unearthed by archeologists.

Once inside the building, he was led to a bathing chamber. The moment he entered, young attendants dressed in ritual robes, both men and women, stepped forward with reverence in their eyes. They guided him towards a sunken pool filled with cool crystal-clear water. The faint scent of lavender and oils hung in the air, soothing his nerves despite the bizarre situation.

When the women started tugging on his clothes, he initially brushed them off, but seeing the distressed look in their eyes stilled him.

They didn't view undressing him as anything other than helping him.

After a moment, Dante allowed himself to be undressed and bathed, which was strange but very relaxing.

He felt like he was being prepared for something—some ritual or ceremony that he couldn't escape.

Once they had removed all the dirt and sand from his hair and body, they left him alone. He leaned back and allowed the water to relax his tired muscles.

He was drifting towards sleep when they returned and helped him out of the tub. Then they dressed him in a fine white chiton, the fabric light yet luxurious against his skin. Gold clasps held the garment in place at his shoulders, and a wide leather belt was fastened around his waist. His feet were slipped into soft leather sandals, and a crown of laurel leaves was placed upon his head.

He guessed that he probably looked like a freaking gladiator except that he didn't have a sword.

The attendants stepped aside, and the village leader reappeared, offering him a subtle nod of approval. "Come. You will dine now."

Dante followed the leader through a series of halls that opened up into a large, open-air dining area. The space was bordered by columns, and beyond them, the view took his breath away. Stretching far into the distance was the shimmering expanse of the sea. The water was impossibly blue, sparkling under the fading light of the setting sun. It was beautiful, almost surreal, like something out of a dream.

He'd always wanted to visit this region. Somehow, coming back in time and seeing it undisturbed by the chaos of the future was even more rewarding.

Then again, he was probably delirious and really just

The Stars

passed out on the hot sand somewhere, dreaming all of this up.

The dinner itself was simple but filling. Fresh fish, olives, bread, and honeyed figs were laid before him. Despite the strange circumstances, Dante found himself eating hungrily, his body finally catching up with the exhaustion of the day. The village leader watched him in silence, occasionally offering a nod but saying little.

When the meal was over, Dante was escorted to a private chamber, high up in the sanctuary. The room was modest but comfortable, with a large bed draped in linen and an open balcony that overlooked the sea. The night breeze drifted in, carrying the scent of salt water and olive trees.

The attendants bowed, then turned and left him alone.

He stood at the edge of the balcony, gazing out at the stars that were beginning to pierce the darkening sky. In the distance on the left, Mount Olympus loomed, ever-present and ominous, like a silent guardian watching over this ancient world. To the right, far below him, was the Aegean Sea.

What was he supposed to do now? He had no map, no plan, and no real understanding of why he was here. The people thought he was Epimetheus, a god from legend, but he was just a man—a man thrust into the past with no idea of what was coming next.

Brea's words haunted him still. "You are the next step in saving this world."

But how? What role did he play in this ancient place, and what fate awaited him?

Dante closed his eyes. His head felt dull and yet was spinning with questions. As the moon rose high in the sky, he wondered if Amy had been sent somewhere as well and if their paths would cross again.

Never in a million years had he imagined his life would take a turn like this. He'd always hoped that Amy would come back into his life. Dreamed of it. He knew that she'd gone down several dark paths since leaving town.

Still, he'd hoped that she'd grow tired of wandering around and dating losers and eventually come home. He had no idea it would mean that he'd end up in a place like this, waiting for her to join him in this primitive paradise.

Watching the last rays of sunlight disappear to the west, he was about to turn towards the massive bed and try to get some rest when he saw a strange purple light coming from the water far below him.

His first thought was that it was a boat, a ship heading in from a long voyage. Then it dawned on him that, while there must be boats in this time, none would have a purple light shining so brightly. Oddly enough, it was heading directly towards him.

Dante froze, his heart pounding in his chest. He gripped the stone edge of the balcony to steady himself. His eyes widened as the purple light hovered just above the water's surface, slowly rising like some kind of ethereal mist. The air around him changed—warmer, electric, like the charge before a storm.

His instincts screamed at him to back away, but his feet remained rooted to the spot. The light moved closer, impossibly graceful, shimmering in the deep hues of twilight. As it ascended higher, the details within the glowing mist started to take form—a figure cloaked in flowing light, delicate and otherworldly.

"Hello, brother," the soft, oddly familiar voice echoed in his mind, not through the air but directly in his thoughts.

His stomach twisted as the realization set in—this was no hallucination. He wasn't imagining it. The voice belonged to Hope, his sister.

But how? How could she be here?

The figure grew clearer, the purple mist dissipating to reveal her. Her features were as he remembered, but sharper, more refined, as if shaped by something greater than time. She floated just beyond the balcony's railing, her long, dark hair swirling around her in a haze of violet light. Her eyes, once warm and comforting, now glowed with a strange luminescence, a reflection of the power coursing through her.

"Hope?" Dante whispered, his voice strained. "What in the hell?" She was supposed to be at a dance school in New York. The last time he'd seen her, she'd just gotten the lead in a holiday production.

The familiarity of her face contrasted so violently with the sheer impossibility of the situation that it left him disoriented. She looked like his sister but not entirely. She was something else, something more.

Long flowing purple fabric swirled around her like clouds and mist as she hovered hundreds of feet above the ground. Her eyes were impossibly violet in color. Her long dark hair flowed in perfect ringlets around her face.

She was the spitting image of how their mother had once looked, long before the cancer had taken her years before he'd graduated high school.

"You've finally come home," Hope repeated, her voice filled with both sorrow and something he couldn't quite place. Relief? Expectation?

Home? What did she mean by that? He wasn't home—he was in ancient Greece, thrust into the past by forces he couldn't understand. The same forces, it seemed, that had taken Hope and turned her into... this.

The wind stirred around them, carrying with it the scent of the sea. His mind raced with questions, memories flooding back.

"How are you here?" he demanded, his voice stronger now, though his pulse was hammering in his ears with fear and confusion.

Hope tilted her head slightly, her expression soft but distant, as if the answers she carried were too heavy for words. "I've always been here, waiting for you. Waiting for this moment."

His chest tightened as he stepped closer to the railing. "What are you talking about? Waiting for what?"

"For you to fulfill your destiny," she replied calmly, as if it were the most obvious thing in the world. "For you to become who you were always meant to be. Your journey has only just begun."

Dante shook his head, frustration mingling with disbelief. "What journey? None of this makes sense. Why did Brea send me here? Why are you here?"

Hope's glowing eyes softened and, for a moment, the ethereal light around her dimmed, revealing more of the sister he remembered—the one who had played with him when they were kids, who always had a smile for him no matter how hard things got. But this version of her felt beyond his reach, like she was more of an idea than the person he once knew.

"All will be revealed in time," she said, her voice distant, almost mechanical. "There are forces at play you cannot comprehend yet. You must trust what you feel."

"What I feel?" Dante nearly laughed, bitterness creeping into his voice. "I feel like I've been thrown into a nightmare I can't wake up from. And now you're telling me I'm supposed to just go along with it?"

Hope reached out her hand towards him, palm open. A gentle wave of purple energy shimmered between them, beckoning him to take her hand.

"You have a choice, brother," she said softly, "but the fate of everything depends on what you do next."

His heart clenched at her words. The fate of everything? He didn't know what to believe anymore. His life had been turned upside down in a matter of hours, and now his sister—this glowing apparition of his sister—was asking him to trust in something he didn't understand.

He hesitated, his hand twitching at his side.

"Dante." Hope's voice softened to a whisper. "You've always known deep down that you're part of something bigger. Now is the time to embrace it."

Dante's jaw tightened as he stared at the hand reaching out to him, the violet glow casting shadows across his face. He wanted to believe her—wanted to believe that somehow there was a purpose to all of this, that everything would eventually make sense. But trust was hard to come by when the world felt so upside down.

"What if I don't want any part of this?" he asked quietly, meeting her eyes.

Hope's expression didn't change, but the glow around her flickered for a brief moment.

"Then everything... will perish."

Chapter Seven

Amy stood in the doorway, staring at one of the smaller rooms off the main silo area. The entire area had been transformed into a makeshift living space for those who remained.

The memories of sneaking into the silo with friends, tagging the walls with spray paint during their rebellious streaks, felt like a lifetime ago. The rawness of her old self, bold and carefree, contrasted so sharply with the quiet desolation she now felt. The soft blue color that the walls had been painted, covering all the old names and art that had once littered the walls, seemed out of place. She was sure that they offered some a sense of comfort, a layer of warmth amidst the bleakness of everything that had happened. All that she had been absent for.

She heard footsteps approaching and turned to see Joe walking in, his face worn and etched with lines she didn't remember on him before. He wasn't the same carefree brother she'd left behind. There was a heaviness in his eyes, one she couldn't place. Behind him, three children shyly shuffled into the room—two identical girls and a boy.

Her heart melted at seeing the mixture of her brother and their mother in their faces.

"This is Luna, Stella, and Orion." His voice was softer than she'd expected, his gaze flicking from her to his three kids. "Kids, this is your aunt Amy."

Luna and Stella, identical with long dirty blonde hair and wide blue eyes, looked up at her with curiosity. They were the spitting image of their mother, Liz—now gone. The sight of them hit her like a punch to the gut. For a moment, Amy couldn't speak, her throat constricting with the memory of Liz, her warmth, her laughter, all lost to the chaos Joe had only begun to hint at.

Had it only been moments since she'd seen the very pregnant Liz standing in the moonlight next to Joe?

Orion stood slightly apart from his sisters, his expression serious, a mirror of Joe's face in his younger years. The boy had Joe's strong jawline, his piercing eyes, and a quiet intensity that unsettled Amy. Seeing the three of them, her brother's kids—Liz's kids—alive in this broken world made everything feel even more surreal.

"Hi," Amy managed, her voice cracking slightly as she crouched slightly to meet them at eye level. "It's so good to meet you."

Luna and Stella smiled shyly, while Orion simply nodded, still sizing her up.

"We've heard a lot about you," Luna said, stepping closer. "Dad told us stories."

Stella piped up, "He said you used to sneak into this room and draw on the walls."

Amy chuckled, glancing at the now pristine walls, a bittersweet smile on her face. "Yeah, I did. I used to get in a lot of trouble for it, too."

Joe's smile widened, though his eyes remained distant. "She was the troublemaker," he added lightly, though the momentary levity couldn't mask the weight of everything else in the room.

"Where have you been?" Orion asked, breaking into the happy silence.

"Son, we've talked about this. Brea sent her here, to her future," Joe said a little firmly.

Amy nodded and gave the boy all of her attention. "Believe it or not, I just left your parents less than an hour ago. Your mother was still this big." She held out her hand to show the kids how large Liz had been. "Carrying the three of you." She glanced at her brother. "Of course, none of us knew at the time that there were three of you."

Joe shrugged. "We wanted it to be a surprise."

For the next hour, Amy spent time with the kids. Luna and Stella stuck close together, talking animatedly about the games they played, the books they read, and how they helped around the underground compound. Orion, however, remained more reserved, his eyes flicking between his sisters and Amy, though he eventually warmed up to her, showing her the small, carved wooden animals he'd made.

The presence of the children, their innocence, was a reminder of the devastation that had torn their world apart. Amy laughed with them, momentarily forgetting the horrors Joe had hinted at, until finally, the questions she'd been avoiding weighed too heavily on her mind.

She looked at Joe, who had been sitting quietly, watching them. "Can we talk? I need to know what happened."

Joe's face tightened. He glanced at the kids, and with a

simple request, he sent them out of the room. "Go see if Brea needs help with dinner," he said gently. Luna and Stella obeyed without question, though Orion remained for a moment, his gaze lingering on his father before he finally left, closing the door behind him.

The room fell into a tense silence. Amy leaned back, her pulse quickening as Joe stood up, rubbing his hand across the back of his neck, as if trying to figure out where to begin.

"It all started after the kids were born," he began, his voice raw with emotion. "About a month after their birth, October tenth, everything went to hell." His eyes darkened as he continued. "Moros—one of the primordial gods—led the attack. He wasn't alone. He gathered other gods, demi-gods, and forces we didn't even know existed. Including Thanatos. The two of them led an army. They came with fury, with destruction."

Amy swallowed hard, trying to process his words. Gods? Demi-gods? It sounded like something out of a nightmare, yet here they were, living it. She could see the pain etched in her brother's face as he spoke, his hands balling into fists at his sides.

"We fought back," Joe said, his jaw tightening. "All of us—me, Michael, Jess, Brea—we did everything we could to protect our world. It was decided that Xtina and Liz would bring all the kids here—Xtina and Michael's daughter, Harper; Brea and Ethan's son, Milo; Jacob and Jess's son Reed; and as many of the townspeople who would follow them while we fought them off. But then they shattered the moon. When it broke, the pieces rained down on the planet, causing earthquakes, tidal waves, and fires. The whole world went into chaos. Countries believed others had attacked and shot off nukes in retaliation. Half the population was killed by the other half. Only small pockets of people survived those first few weeks."

Amy's heart sank, her mind flashing to the empty streets, the hollow world she'd walked through on her way to find them. "That's why everything's so... quiet?"

Joe nodded, his eyes distant. "Everything changed after that. There are pockets of survivors, people who've banded together, but most are gone now, disbursed after years of starvation or fighting amongst themselves. More than half of the planet is dead. More than half." He rested his head in his hands.

Amy felt a wave of nausea rise in her throat, her hands shaking slightly as she gripped the edge of the small table. She thought of all the people that she used to know, the families, friends... gone. "And Liz?"

Joe's expression faltered for the first time, his eyes clouding over with grief. "Liz... she didn't make it through the first battle. She died protecting the kids when they came for them." Joe's gaze moved to the door. "If Xtina hadn't been there..." He shook his head. "She's the only reason all of the kids are alive."

The air in the room felt thick and oppressive. Amy's chest tightened as the tears welled up in her eyes, threatening to spill over. She bit her lip, trying to keep herself composed.

"But they survived," Joe continued, his voice barely above a whisper. "Luna, Stella, Orion... they're the last part of her. They survived."

Amy wiped at her eyes, nodding, though her heart ached. She had so many other questions, so much she wanted to understand, but the weight of Joe's story—of everything that had happened—was too much to process all at once. She could tell he was tired. Knew that just retelling how he'd lost everything weighed heavy on him.

"Why didn't you tell me you had powers sooner?" she whispered. "What your group of friends could do?"

Joe looked away, his jaw tight. "I wanted to, but the others felt that we couldn't risk it. Not until now. Not until..." He paused, his voice trailing off as if he were about to say something he wasn't ready to.

Amy stood up, crossing the room to stand beside her brother. "Until what?"

Joe exhaled deeply, meeting her eyes with a mixture of guilt and determination. "Until we knew what you were capable of."

"What I'm capable of?" She shook her head, not understanding his meaning.

"Brea has seen it all. She's gone further into the future, hundreds of years beyond this. She has traveled to different timelines where this didn't happen. Where they used different methods to destroy things or where they never attacked." He motioned to the room. "Each of those times, you're the first key to unlocking what lets us win, you and Dante. That's why..." He shook his head and closed his eyes. "I can't tell you anything more. I'm not..." He sighed and rolled his shoulders, a move she remembered her brother making so many times before. "Before the sun rises, you'll leave us again." His eyes locked with hers. "This time, you will go because of your powers."

She frowned.

"Did you ever wonder why I never left Hidden Creek?" he asked suddenly. The change of subject threw her off.

"N-no."

Her brother smiled slightly for the first time. Then to her utter shock, he flew across the room so fast that his body was nothing but a streak of colors. Before she had a chance to blink, he was back, sitting in the chair across from her with a soda can in his hand, sipping the drink.

She had believed she'd imagined him moving so fast that night she'd left. Imagined that everything she and Dante had witnessed had been faked somehow.

"Oh, my bad, did you want one too?" he said and—zip!—a soda can appeared on the table in front of her.

"Speed." He sighed. "My gift is speed. I spent years trying to escape Hidden Creek. I'd travel far away, but I always ended up back here. Because I was tied to this place. My fate has always been here. Each of us here has powers. Our survival depends on it."

She frowned as she reached out and touched the cold drink to make sure it was there.

"Xtina, well, you've heard all about hers for years. The rumors are very much true. Jess really is a witch. Remember seeing her fly? And, well, there's more to her than the light show." He smirked. "A damned good witch. Brea, well, she can teleport herself and others through time and worlds. You probably caught onto that one." He chuckled.

She nodded slightly, then opened the drink and took a long sip.

"Joleen can control time and space, sort of. Among other things. Tara and Selene are pretty much indestructible and can fly, remember?"

She nodded. "Mia is a djinn," she said in a distant voice as she remembered.

He nodded. "Yes, and Lucas is a shifter."

"The dog?" she asked.

"Cerberus."

"Seriously? The hellhound?" She balked.

He shrugged. "Ethan can heal others, Jacob can control

anyone or anything that he locks eyes with, and I have speed."

Her head was spinning with all the details.

"What about Liz?" She had meant to ask if Liz believed all of this but was shocked when Joe replied.

"Liz was our oracle. She'd foreseen all of this ahead of time. She knew the exact moment…" He closed his eyes. "The exact moment she was going to die. She warned me. Tried to prepare me for what was to come. She is the reason you were sent here first instead of into the past along with Dante."

"Where is Dante?" she asked, feeling her heart dip in her chest.

Joe's gaze moved up to hers. "Greece. About three thousand years in the past."

She blinked a few times. "Why there?"

Joe chuckled, a dry sort of helpless sound. "It's where it all starts."

"Where what starts?"

Joe shifted slightly. "Your legend."

"My… what?"

"The story of Pandora… You." Joe took a sip of his drink.

Amy stared at her brother, her mind spinning as the words settled in. "Pandora? Me?"

Joe nodded, his face a mixture of pride and sorrow. "It wasn't just a story, Amy. It was a prophecy, one that stretches back through the centuries. Every world and every timeline has its version of Pandora. But here, in our time, it's you."

She blinked, the weight of everything beginning to press down on her chest. "I don't understand. The story of some goddess with a stupid box that holds…what? Hope or the world's destruction? What does that have to do with me?"

The Stars

Joe leaned back, running a hand through his disheveled hair. "Pandora was more than just a woman who opened some mythical box. She was the key to unlocking worlds—both creation and destruction. The gods knew it. The box... the legend, it was never about unleashing evil into the world. It was about balance, about tipping the scales between life and death, hope and despair."

Amy's heart raced as she tried to process it all. "And Dante..."

"Dante's fate is tied to yours," Joe said, his voice heavy with responsibility. "He's your balance, your counterpart. He's Epimetheus. It's why Brea sent you on separate paths. You have to find him in Greece, and you will discover your full potential there. But first, you must start the process of awakening here."

She stood, the room suddenly feeling too small, too suffocating. "And these... powers I'm supposed to have. What are they?"

"Who knows? Soon, with Dante's help, you will discover them. You'll remember who you are. Liz saw it all. Besides, Mia has met you in another world." Amy remembered the flashes of memory Mia had shown her. "You told her there that she would help you remember who you are. Liz prepared me for this, even though I wasn't ready to accept it. None of us were. But you were born for this. We all were." Joe's eyes darkened. "Moros and the other gods—they knew what was coming. That's why they attacked, why they shattered the moon. They fear what you can become. They just didn't know that Brea had sent you away before it all began. They fear you. Fear what you can do."

Amy's knees felt weak, her pulse thundering in her ears. "Fear... me?"

Joe nodded, his expression grim. "Because... you're the

only one who can undo everything they've put into motion. You're the only one who can save this world."

The enormity of her brother's words settled over her like a cold weight, pressing down on her shoulders until she could hardly breathe. She wasn't just Amy anymore. She wasn't just a girl thrown into a future that she didn't understand.

She was Pandora.

Chapter Eight

Dante had lost track of time. Days passed in a haze, blending like sand in the wind. The people of Thessalia treated him as though he were a deity, bowing, offering him food, and whispering prayers when they thought he wasn't listening. But despite the reverence, he felt nothing but isolation. No one dared speak to him directly, except the village leader, who would visit each evening to ensure his "needs" were met. Dante's so-called "freedom" was confined to the luxurious temple chambers and the surrounding courtyard. There were ever-present servants to make sure that he never crossed the threshold into the streets.

Hope came and went as she pleased every evening, always in that mystical form—purple light shimmering in the night, her voice soft but commanding. She was there, but not there. Like a dream, she appeared when the sunset and the village quieted, leaving Dante alone with his thoughts. He had tried explaining her presence to the temple leader, but his words were dismissed as divine visions meant only for him.

"Your path is guided by the gods," the leader had said, bowing deeply. "It is not for us mortals to interfere."

It was frustrating. He wasn't a god. He wasn't divine. He was just a man, a police officer, trapped in a time he didn't understand, waiting for answers that never seemed to come. He had tried to press Hope for more information, but she would simply smile, her form dissolving into the mist as quickly as it had come.

On the seventh night, Dante stood on the balcony once again, watching the sea. The moon's pale reflection shimmered on the water, casting an ethereal glow across the horizon. His thoughts drifted to Amy, wondering where she was and if she was safe. He had no idea what was happening back in his own time, but he couldn't shake the feeling that she'd soon be there. That she was supposed to be with him.

"Brother." The soft voice filled his mind again.

He turned to see Hope materializing before him, the familiar swirl of purple mist solidifying into her form.

"You've been quiet," he said, crossing his arms. "Not much for conversation these last few nights."

Hope smiled faintly. "I have been watching, waiting. Your time here is coming to an end."

Dante frowned. "What do you mean?"

"You are not meant to stay in Thessalia. Your path leads elsewhere," she said, her voice as calm as ever. "Tomorrow, at first light, you will travel to Delos Island."

"Delos?" The name rang with a distant familiarity, something he vaguely recalled from a long-forgotten history or geography class. "Why Delos?"

Hope's glowing eyes met his. "There, you will find Pandora. You must awaken her."

Pandora. The name hit him like a punch to the gut, dredging up a thousand questions all at once. Pandora—the woman who had unleashed the evils of the world in ancient myth. The one cursed by the gods. What did she have to do with his own life, his time?

"Why me?" he asked, his voice quieter now, unsure. "What does Pandora have to do with me?"

Hope's smile faltered for a brief moment, her gaze softening. "You are more connected to her than you know. But that knowledge will come in time."

"Why can't you just tell me now?" he asked, frustration creeping into his voice. "Why all the cryptic messages? I'm flying blind here."

"You will understand when you reach Delos," she said softly. "And when you find Pandora, you will know the truth."

Dante's chest tightened, anxiety clawing at the edges of his mind. The weight of everything—being called a god, trapped in this ancient world, and now being tasked with saving someone who was nothing more than a myth—felt too much.

"How am I even supposed to get to Delos?" he asked, voice tense. "I'm not exactly free to roam."

Hope's figure shimmered in the moonlight, her smile returning. "The path will reveal itself. All you need to do is be ready."

He opened his mouth to protest, to demand more answers, but before he could say anything, Hope's form began to dissolve into the purple mist once again.

"Wait!" he shouted, stepping forward. "Hope, wait!"

But it was too late. She was gone, leaving him alone once more with nothing but questions and the cold sea breeze. He clenched his fists in frustration as his mind raced with a million questions.

Delos Island.

Pandora.

He had no choice now. He had to go. And somehow, some way, he would get there.

The next morning, Dante woke to a knock at the heavy wooden door of his chamber. Before he could call out for whoever it was to enter, the door creaked open, revealing the village leader.

The man appeared to be eager. His long white hair was pulled back into a knot at the base of his neck. He was wearing ceremonial robes and had a few more medallions around his neck. There was a gleam of certainty in his eyes, like he held the answers to the universe.

"You must travel to Delos," the leader said, his voice soft but resolute.

Dante sat up, blinking the sleep from his eyes. "How did you—"

"I was shown, just as I was shown of your coming," the leader interrupted, stepping into the room. His gaze never wavered, as if the gods themselves had spoken through him. "I saw it in my dreams. You are to go now to Mount Cythus. There, you will stand before the gods and get guidance."

Dante swung his legs over the side of the bed, his thoughts immediately returning to Hope's cryptic message from the night before. It wasn't a choice anymore. Whatever was happening, he was a part of it.

He dressed quickly with the man standing over him, then the village leader gestured for him to follow, and soon they were walking through the winding pathways of the temple grounds, past tall pillars draped in vines, until they reached the docks. The sun had barely risen, casting a golden glow over the calm waters of the Aegean.

Two sleek, narrow boats waited for them, carved from dark wood and adorned with intricate designs of sea creatures, their eyes and bodies inlaid with shimmering silver. The sails were made from thick linen, painted with symbols of the gods, bright against the pale canvas. A small crew of men, their faces solemn, stood ready by the boats, awaiting the journey ahead.

"You will be safe with them," the leader assured, motioning towards the sailors. "The gods have blessed this passage."

"Why? Why have you helped me?" he asked the man.

"You being here has saved our village from the Fates." He nodded. "What was to come has now been avoided. We thank you." He bowed again. "Safe journey."

Dante nodded, though the word "safe" felt thin and fragile compared to the enormity of everything weighing on him. He climbed into the lead boat, taking a seat at the back while the crew pushed off from the docks.

The boats glided effortlessly through the calm seas, cutting across the water like birds in flight. The wind was light enough to fill the small sails and keep their speed steady. There was a sense of tranquility in the air, as though the world was holding its breath, waiting for something to unfold. The crew barely spoke, their eyes focused on the horizon ahead as if they too sensed the importance of this journey.

Dante watched as the coastline of Thessalia slowly shrank behind them. The waters were a deep sapphire and as they sailed further he could see several small islands dotting the horizon. As they got closer, he noticed that some had jagged cliffs and others a gentler slope to them. He wanted to explore them each and wondered which one they traveled to. However, hours passed as they moved around and beyond those islands.

Soon, the faint outline of Delos appeared in the distance.

He could tell it was their destination, as they were heading directly towards it. The island rose like a crown from the water, its slopes green and fertile. Looming above it all was Mount Cythus, its massive peak a sharp contrast to the flatter lands.

As they neared, he could make out the great temples that dotted the landscape, their white stones gleaming in the sunlight. Marble columns towered over the island, grand structures built in honor of gods that he barely understood.

The boats drifted into a small cove, where a narrow path led up through olive groves and cypress trees towards the heart of the island.

As they made their way up the cove, one of the rowers blew a horn of sorts. Short fast bursts from the land followed in reply. Once they docked, one of the rowers stepped off the boat and handed something to a man who quickly took off towards a building.

Moments later, a different man stepped forward.

It was obvious that this man, another older, gray-haired gentleman dressed almost identically to the other village leader, was the head of this town. The man helped Dante disembark and then pointed towards the mountain. "You will get guidance there. Follow me."

Dante followed the leader and a group of men up the pathway, each step bringing him closer to whatever awaited him near the base of Mount Cythus. Somehow, his unease grew more as the trees thinned and they grew closer to the sprawling temples.

At the foot of the mountain was a massive outdoor theater, carved into the rock itself. Rows and rows of stone seats rose up the hillside in a semi-circle. The place looked capable of holding thousands of people, but today it was empty, save for the whispers of the wind.

The Stars

The village leader stopped just before the entrance to the theater. "This is where you will stand, where the gods speak."

Dante looked all around him. There was a large circular stage in the heart of the amphitheater, surrounded by the empty seats, which seemed to watch him. The vastness of it was overwhelming.

He'd attended several large concerts in his time, but none had ever been in an arena this large.

Were there even this many people on the island? Did people travel from all over to watch plays or fights here?

Who had built this place? From what he could tell, it was older than the town. Centuries older. Had the townspeople found this place and assumed that the gods had built it?

As he watched the leader disappear, he realized that he had expected an audience, maybe a gathering of priests or locals, but here, in the middle of this grand place, there was nothing. Just him and silence.

He stepped forward, his feet carrying him down into the middle of the theater. His footsteps echoed as he approached the center of the stage. By the time he made it there, the sun was hanging high in the sky, casting long shadows across the empty stone seats.

He stood silent for a moment, the calm seas at his back, the high mountain peak hovering ahead of him. Dante had never felt more isolated. Endless questions flooded his mind.

Suddenly, the wind picked up, a soft breeze brushing against his skin, and for a moment he could almost hear whispers. Voices from another time, or maybe another world.

He closed his eyes, took a deep breath, and waited for whatever was to come next.

"What are you doing here," a deep voice boomed so loudly that the ground shook, "out-of-time cop?" The last was a hiss.

Dante opened his eyes and blinked, his heart racing as he took in the sight of a towering figure before him.

There, in front of him, blocking out the view of the mountain, stood a giant. Like, for real. The man was more than three hundred feet tall. His skin was bronzed, and chiseled as though carved from the same marble as the ancient temples around them. He held a massive trident with an odd live creature wrapped around the staff. Both man and creature looked at him, waiting for an answer.

The giant—Prometheus, he realized—loomed over him, his voice vibrating through the stones beneath Dante's feet.

"What in the..." Dante took a few steps back.

"Epimetheus?" The giant's eyes narrowed slightly when Dante spoke. Then Prometheus smiled and a burst of laughter shook the ground once more. "Brother, I did not recognize you."

He shrank to human size, though the force of his presence didn't diminish. Now the oppressive weight of his gaze felt more personal, more pointed.

"Brother?" Dante repeated, his mind spinning. He felt disconnected, caught between this ancient world and his memories. "I'm not... I'm not..." It dawned on him then that the townspeople had called him Epimetheus, who was indeed Prometheus's brother. "Epimetheus," he finished quietly.

Prometheus, now standing at Dante's height, chuckled darkly. "You wear his face, and his essence clings to you like

The Stars

smoke. You may not be Epimetheus in mind, but in soul... you are him, whether you know it or not."

Dante opened his mouth to protest, but Prometheus waved him off, his movements graceful for someone who had once been a hulking giant. "It matters little. Names change. Faces change. But the roles remain the same. You are here for her, are you not?" His voice softened.

Dante frowned. "Her? Pandora?"

Prometheus's eyes darkened, his smile fading into something more dangerous. He stepped closer, his face inches from Dante's now. "Do you know what it is you are about to do?"

Dante swallowed hard but didn't back down. "I'm supposed to find her. To wake her."

"To wake her?" Prometheus's laugh was harsh, filled with something more than mere amusement. "Brother, you are playing with forces you cannot comprehend. Pandora must remain asleep. If she wakes, only ruin will follow. No one can stop what comes next."

Dante shook his head. "But I thought—"

"Thought what?" Prometheus snapped, cutting him off. "That you would find her and everything would be well? That you, together, can save the world? No, brother, it is not that simple. Pandora's slumber is the last barrier between the world you know and utter chaos. She is more than a woman, more than a story—she is a force. And forces like her should never be unleashed."

"But Brea, Hope, they told me I had to save her," Dante said, his voice cracking with uncertainty.

"Hope." Prometheus spat the name like venom. "You mean Elpis." His eyes narrowed again. "Elpis, like so many others, believes too easily in the promise of redemption. But you, you must understand—this is not about saving Pandora.

It is about keeping her locked away. She carries the weight of destruction. If she wakes, the world as you know it will burn. It will collapse under the weight of her burden. It always has."

"What burden?" he asked, wondering if he wanted to know the answer.

"To save all." Prometheus sighed.

Dante's throat tightened. His mind reeled as he tried to piece together the puzzle. "But if she's asleep, doesn't that mean everyone dies anyway?"

Prometheus looked at him for a long moment, his expression unreadable. "There are those who still believe in redemption. They think they can control the uncontrollable. That they can fix what was broken so long ago. But I am telling you, brother—Pandora is not the solution. She is the end. The end to you. To all of us."

Dante felt a wave of doubt wash over him. "So what do I do?"

Prometheus took a step back, his eyes flashing with warning. "You let her sleep. You turn away from the path they've set for you. If you wake her, you will unleash not only her curse but the fury of some of the gods. They will not forgive. They will not show mercy. In time, they will come for her and you."

Dante clenched his fists at his sides. "But what if she's the only way to stop this? What if I don't have a choice?"

Prometheus's gaze softened, but the danger in his voice remained. "There is always a choice, brother. Always. You can choose to leave her in peace, to let the world keep its fragile balance. Or you can wake her and watch everything crumble around you. The rest of the gods will not intervene. They will only watch as the chaos unfolds."

Dante's breath came in short, shallow bursts as he

The Stars

processed Prometheus's words. He had been sent here to find Pandora, to wake her, to somehow save this world. But now, standing before someone who had seen the consequences of such actions, doubt gnawed at him.

Prometheus stepped closer again, placing a firm hand on Dante's shoulder. "I have warned you. I have done what I can. The rest is up to you. But mark my words, brother—Pandora must not be unleashed. Let her sleep."

With that, Prometheus turned and began to walk away, his figure fading into the shadows of the massive amphitheater. Dante was left alone. Every instinct told him that the stakes were higher than he could imagine and that his decision here would ripple through time and worlds in ways he couldn't yet understand.

He closed his eyes again, feeling the cool wind brush against his skin. The path ahead was uncertain, and Prometheus's warning echoed in his mind, but somewhere deep within him, there was a pull—a pull.

Dante opened his eyes and looked out at the empty seats of the theater, his heart pounding in his chest.

What in the hell did he know?

Chapter Nine

After Joe showed her back into the main silo area, where a group of people gathered to eat a meal, Amy sat in silence, mulling over everything he'd just told her. She recognized almost everyone in the dark, damp place.

There were kids of all ages running around with a soccer ball, playing quietly after the meal. Her nieces and nephew were among the ranks.

She sat with her knees drawn up, her back resting against the cold, curved wall of the silo. The dim lighting from the few oil lamps scattered across the room, casting a flickering glow on the faces around her—old friends, family members, people that she had once lived among before everything had gone so horribly wrong. Now they were huddled together—tired, skinny, weak—sharing a somber meal, trying to carve out some normalcy in this bleak, underground refuge.

Her thoughts kept circling back to what Joe had said. Moros. The gods. Pandora.

What in the hell was happening? Was all this real or was she dreaming?

Just as she was about to get up and find a moment of solitude, someone sat beside her.

She recognized Hope, Dante's younger sister, immediately. Her presence was as quiet and mysterious as always. Amy hadn't seen her since she'd graduated from high school. The last that she'd heard, Hope was in New York, studying to be a dancer.

"Remember me?" Hope asked as she gave her a small smile. Amy nodded. "I thought you might want to talk," she said softly, pulling her knees up to match Amy's posture.

Amy glanced at her, unsure where to start. "How... you were in New York."

Hope nodded. "I came home after Dante disappeared, after the two of you disappeared on the same night. At first, those of us that didn't believe them"—she motioned towards Xtina and the rest—"thought that the two of you had run off together." She sighed and rested her head back as she glanced up at the top of the silo's massive cover. "I was so angry. Our dad died not knowing the truth." She shook her head and wiped a tear from her cheek. "Then, after the attack, everyone started believing their crazy stories."

"Stories?" Amy asked.

Hope glanced over at her. "That the two of you were sent somewhere to stop this all from happening. When I saw you walk in here, looking not a day older than the last time I'd seen you, I knew." She frowned. "But Dante's not with you?"

Amy shook her head. "Not... yet." She shrugged.

"I didn't think I'd survive," Hope admitted. "When the first wave hit, I'd just come home. Then the world was in chaos. We couldn't hold the line. Most of us scattered." She looked around the silo, her gaze lingering on the people huddled in small groups. "These are the last of us, Amy. We're tired."

Amy's throat tightened. "What are you saying? That you're going to run?"

Hope turned her head sharply, meeting Amy's eyes with a defiant spark. "I won't run. None of us will. We'll fight... and when we can't fight anymore, we'll hide until we can fight again. That's what survivors do." She turned slightly towards her. "So, the question is, what are you going to do? What are you and my brother going to do to stop all of this from happening?"

Before Amy could respond, the ground beneath them shuddered. It started subtly, like the trembling of a distant earthquake. But within moments, the tremor grew, sending ripples through the metal walls of the silo.

Amy bolted upright. "What was that?"

Hope stood too, her eyes wide with recognition. "No... it's too soon," she whispered, her face going pale. "They've found us."

Before Amy could ask who, a deafening screech tore through the air, and the ceiling of the silo—the massive dome above them—began to peel back, as though it were nothing more than the lid of a tin can.

A scream erupted around them. Everyone scrambled for cover as chunks of debris began to rain down on them. Amy's heart raced as she looked up. A swirling mass of darkness hovered above the silo. She saw ugly creatures circling around a dark figure that was descending towards them.

"Moros," Hope whispered, her voice trembling. "He's here."

Amy's blood ran cold. She had never seen a god before,

but the stories that her brother had told her were enough to instill fear in her.

Moros, the god of doom and darkness, circled above them, surrounded by winged, shadowy figures—his army of Harpies or demi-gods. Their eyes gleamed red as they swooped into the silo, cutting through the panicked crowd like a storm of death.

In a single wave, half of the people inside were struck down. Bodies fell around Amy, lifeless before they even hit the ground. The air was filled with screams of terror and the metallic scent of blood.

"Xtina! Jess!" Hope screamed, her voice cracking. Amy turned just in time to see her friends—Xtina, Jess, and the others—band together, trying to form a circle of defense against the onslaught. Xtina's and Jess's bodies glowed with power, the air around them sparking with electricity. Jess's hands weaved intricate patterns, casting spells of protection as fast as her fingers could move, shooting lightning bolts from her fingertips. Mia shifted into the massive dragon, while Lucas changed into a huge black three-headed dog and took out half a dozen of the demi-gods with one blow.

But it wasn't enough. One by one, they were struck down, their bodies collapsing in brutal flashes of light.

Amy's breath came in ragged gasps as the horror unfolded before her eyes. She turned, desperate to find Joe, her nieces, and her nephew. And there they were—Luna, Stella, Orion—all lying injured and bleeding, struggling to move, or already dead. Joe hovered over them, tears in his eyes as he screamed.

"No!" The word tore from her throat, but her legs felt heavy, her body rooted in place by fear. She couldn't reach them. She couldn't help them.

Hope grabbed her arm, pulling her closer. "Amy, listen

to me!" she yelled. "You have to run! There's nothing you can do! Not during this time."

But something snapped deep inside her. The sight of the children—their small, fragile bodies lying broken—triggered something deep within her, something primal, something she couldn't contain.

Her body shook violently, a surge of energy bubbling up inside her from deep down. She felt it building, pressing against the very fabric of her being, desperate to be released.

"Amy—" Hope's voice was distant like it was being swallowed by the roaring storm around them. But Amy couldn't hear anything clearly anymore. The power was too loud. Too demanding.

She opened her mouth, and a scream erupted from her —a scream so powerful, so filled with raw energy, that the very air around them seemed to tremble.

Moros and his army faltered.

The dark Harpies and demi-gods staggered mid-flight, their shadows flickering as if struggling to hold their form. Moros turned his golden glowing gaze onto her, his expression twisting into one of recognition, then surprise, and finally... fear.

The god of doom, the bringer of darkness, the destroyer of worlds, feared her.

Amy collapsed to her knees, the energy still pulsing within her but less violently now, more controlled. She panted, her body drenched in sweat, her heart pounding like a war drum.

"Pandora..." Moros's voice was a low rumble, filled with rage and something else. Dread. In one quick move, his hands rose and pointed directly at her. A bright flash. A quick burst of pain.

Amy's vision blurred, her body heavy as she collapsed

onto the rocky ground. Her limbs trembled from the force of Moros' attack, his dark power coursing through her veins like poison. Everything around her seemed to fade into nothingness—except for one thought.

Dante.

She was supposed to see Dante again.

"I will stop you," she whispered, her voice trembling. She tried to summon the strength to stand, but her body betrayed her.

Power pulsed from Moros and shot straight towards her again. She heard screaming, felt pain like she'd never felt before. Then, darkness crept into her vision. Moros' sinister grin was the last thing she saw before everything went black.

When Amy awoke, the world around her was still. The sound of distant birds singing and a soft warm breeze caressing her face felt surreal after the chaos she'd just escaped. The first thing she noticed was a face—a young boy, perhaps no older than ten, peering down at her with wide, curious eyes.

"Are you alive?" the boy asked, his voice full of concern and wonder.

Amy's throat was dry as she tried to respond. "Where...? Where am I?"

"You're at the base of Mount Cythus," the boy said, his words gentle as he reached down to help her sit up. His hands were small but surprisingly strong. "You appeared out of nowhere. Are you a goddess? Are you hurt? I didn't know gods could get hurt." He frowned slightly.

She tried to speak but winced as a sharp pain shot through her chest. She was weak, too weak to fight back if Moros returned. She needed time to recover, to get to Dante. She had to...

The Stars

"Theo," the boy said, introducing himself with a warm smile. "My name is Theo. I'm a farmer, well, a goat herder. Are you a goddess?" he asked again.

Amy blinked, unsure how to respond to that question. Her mind was hazy, still reeling from the battle. "No... I'm... I'm just..."

Theo's eyes widened as he glanced down at something beside her. Amy followed his gaze and saw her cell phone, which had fallen from her coat pocket, lying in the dirt beside her. It had slipped out without her noticing. Theo looked at it in awe, as though it were some sacred artifact.

"Is this box... from the gods?" Theo whispered, reverently picking up the phone and holding it up to her.

Amy managed a weak chuckle. "Not exactly." She leaned her back against a rock and reached out with shaky hands to unlock her phone screen. The brightness momentarily blinded her, but the familiar images of her world flickered across the screen—pictures of her friends, her family, and moments that felt like they belonged to a different lifetime.

Theo gasped as he stared at the images. "You can see into the future? Are these other worlds? Are these all gods?"

Amy smiled faintly, too tired to explain the complexities of technology. Instead, she swiped through the photos, showing Theo snapshots of her world. His face was a mixture of awe and disbelief, his young mind struggling to comprehend what he was seeing.

"Are these the other gods?" Theo asked again, pointing at a photo of Dante, unaware of the connection between them.

Amy's heart tightened at the sight of her brother's face as he and Dante posed for the photo. She nodded slowly. "In a way, yes."

Theo knelt beside her, his eyes wide with admiration. "You must be here to meet with the other gods. The gods don't send people like you unless it's to save us."

Amy's breath hitched. Save us. She wasn't sure she was ready for that responsibility. She wasn't even sure she could do it. But as she sat there, staring at her phone and at Theo, something stirred within her. The pain in her chest subsided just a little.

"Can you help me?" she said softly, her voice and her mind a little steadier now. If Dante was already here, would they think he was a god too? Would they have taken him somewhere where the gods meet? "Can you show me where the other gods would meet?"

Theo nodded eagerly. "Of course. It's not far. I'll take you."

Amy leaned on him for support as they started their slow journey towards the town. Each step was a struggle, her body still aching, but Theo's presence—his kindness—helped her push through most of the pain.

As they walked, Theo kept glancing at the phone in her hands, as though it were a piece of divine magic. He didn't ask any more questions, perhaps sensing that she was too tired to answer.

Dante was out here, somewhere. And somehow, they would find each other. Somehow they had to stop that horrible future from happening.

After all, Joe had mentioned that Brea had gone to many different futures. Different possibilities. Did that mean nothing was set in stone? Could she and Dante really change what she'd seen?

As they neared the outskirts of the town, Amy felt her strength returning—slowly but surely. Whatever Moros had

The Stars

done to her, she wasn't going to let it stop her. Not now. Not when so much was at stake.

As Theo led Amy through the bustling village streets, she noticed curious glances from the villagers who eyed her. She was here for something beyond their understanding, and even though Theo had been kind, Amy felt a deep sense of isolation growing inside her.

The buildings around them gradually gave way to an open space. The air felt different here—charged, heavy with something ancient. As they approached the base of Mount Cythus, Amy's heart raced. The mountain loomed overhead, its jagged peaks cutting into the sky like the teeth of some great beast. There was an energy here, one she could feel thrumming beneath her skin, and it filled her with both anticipation and dread.

Theo stopped suddenly and pointed up the mountain path. "There," he said, his voice quiet, as though he too could feel the presence of something far greater than either of them. "The theater is just beyond those trees. The gods speak to others there. I'm not allowed to go beyond this point."

Amy swallowed hard, nodding. She had no idea what she was walking into, but she knew she had no choice. Dante was here. Somewhere. She could feel it. And the gods... She wasn't sure what their plans were for either of them, but she knew they couldn't turn back now.

"Thank you, Theo," she whispered, placing a hand on the boy's shoulder. His eyes lit up and he smiled shyly before running back towards the village, leaving her alone on the path.

The climb was steeper than she'd expected, every step reminding her how weak she still felt. But determination pushed her forward. The wind picked up as she neared the top of the pathway, swirling around her like unseen hands trying to pull her back.

Finally, the path opened into a grand amphitheater carved into the mountainside. It was immense, larger than anything she'd ever seen. The seats seemed to stretch on forever, rows upon rows of stone benches climbing towards the sky. At the center of it all, standing alone in the middle of the stage, was Dante.

Amy's breath caught in her throat when she saw him, his silhouette striking against the backdrop of the ancient stone. He was staring up at the sky, lost in thought, the tension in his body palpable even from a distance.

Her heart leaped at the sight of him. He looked small from where she stood at the edge of the theater, but she could feel the power radiating from him even from this distance. He wasn't the same Dante she remembered. Something had changed.

She took a step forward, her voice catching in her throat. "Dante..."

He turned slowly, his eyes meeting hers across the vast expanse. For a moment, there was nothing but silence between them. The world seemed to hold its breath as they stared at each other, two pieces of a puzzle that had been separated for far too long.

"Amy," Dante breathed, his voice laced with relief and something else—something deeper.

She stepped onto the stone stage, her legs trembling beneath her. "Dante..."

Before she could say more, the weight of everything—the attack, the injuries, the overwhelming journey—hit her all at once. She staggered, feeling the world spin around her, and Dante was there in an instant, catching her before she collapsed.

The Stars

"Are you alright?" he asked, his voice laced with concern. He looked over her face, his hand steadying her by the waist.

Amy blinked, forcing herself to focus. "I'm here. I made it. I didn't have a choice," she said. "Moros—he's coming. He's... killed everyone."

"Killed?" He frowned.

"In the... future." She shook her head. "We have to change it."

He moved them over until they were sitting on one of the stone seats. "I've spoken with Prometheus."

"Prometheus... the Titan?" she asked.

Dante nodded. "He warned me not to wake Pandora. He said that no good would come of it. I have no idea where Pandora is or even how to wake her. So I don't think that will be a problem." He sighed.

Amy's blood ran cold. She turned towards him until their eyes locked.

"Dante, I am Pandora."

Chapter Ten

Dante met her gaze. The shock and truth of what she was telling him hit him square in the chest.

"You... you're Pandora?" He frowned.

She closed her eyes for a moment. "I'm... tired," she said suddenly. "How long have you been here?" she asked after her eyes ran over his clothing.

"Days." He shook his head. "A week." He didn't know really. He'd lost track of time.

"For me, it's been about eight hours since we stood in that field and I watched you disappear. I haven't slept since. Do you think this"—she motioned between them—"can wait?"

He nodded, then quickly stood up and helped her stand. He kept his gaze on her as they made their way down the stone steps of the theater, her weight heavy against him. She was weak, barely holding herself together after whatever hell she had just gone through, but the stubbornness in her eyes told him she wouldn't give up. He admired that, even if it terrified him to see her so drained. They needed time—time to rest, time to think.

As they descended the steps, a figure emerged at the edge of the theater—the silver-haired town leader. His eyes were sharp and calculating, but there was a reverence in the way he looked at Dante and Amy, like he'd been waiting there for them.

"She is the one the gods have sent for you," the man said softly, his voice calm but filled with certainty. When Dante nodded, the man motioned. "Come with me. You must need rest."

Amy's breaths were coming in short, ragged gasps. She nodded slightly, and they followed the man down a narrow path into the village. A small boy appeared, and Amy quickly mentioned that this was Theo, the boy who had found her and showed her the way to him. The boy nodded to him in greeting and then walked quietly behind them.

As they walked down the streets of the village, people were going about their daily tasks, and they stopped and watched them pass by. They parted for them, creating a clear path for them to walk. The whispers followed them like they were something otherworldly. He'd seen this kind of reverence before, felt it in the way people looked at him, thinking he was something more than human. It felt like a burden.

The town's leader led them to a large, elegant house set apart from the others. The building stood beneath the shade of towering olive trees, its white walls gleaming in the late afternoon sun. Dante could smell the faint scent of freshly baked bread and herbs as they neared the entrance. He glanced at Amy and she looked as if she could barely keep her eyes open at this point.

"You will be safe here," the man said, opening the door and ushering them inside.

The Stars

The cool air hit Dante's skin as they stepped over the threshold, the peaceful quiet of the house a stark contrast to the buzzing energy outside. Inside, the home was simple yet beautiful, the stone walls adorned with delicate tapestries. The floors were covered with large colorful handwoven rugs.

"I'll show you to your rooms," the man said, leading them further into the house.

Amy was taken into a private room, and Dante paused for a moment as he watched her make her way inside. She needed rest. Badly. He could see the strain in her movements, the way her shoulders slumped, and it gnawed at him. But he also knew that this was Amy—she couldn't be broken easily. He remembered how strong and outspoken she'd been in school. How she'd stood up to bullies and fought for the weaker kids in grade school. It was one of the first things he'd liked about her.

A woman appeared, a soft-spoken servant, and she gently guided Amy towards a large stone tub. The door closed behind them, leaving Dante standing alone in the hallway.

He replayed Prometheus's warning. And now, Amy was here with him. She was Pandora. Pandora.

He ran a hand through his hair. They needed to figure out what to do next, and how to stop what she said was coming, thousands of years from now.

Prometheus had warned him not to wake Pandora, but he couldn't shake the feeling that things were already in motion, far beyond his control. If Amy was Pandora, then why did he have to wake her? How? What did that mean? Was there something more to do to transform her into Pandora?

The scent of food drifted from down the hall, pulling him from his thoughts. Dante followed it into a large room where a table was set with platters of food—bread, meats, fruits, cheeses—all fresh and waiting. He realized how hungry he was, how long it had been since he'd eaten. He dropped into a chair, grabbed a piece of bread, and tore into it.

He ate in silence for a while, trying to shake off the weariness that clung to him, but his mind was restless. Just as he was about to reach for more food, the door opened, and Amy stepped in.

She was dressed in a pale blue gown, and her long damp hair was neatly braided back. She looked cleaner, more composed, but there was still a tiredness in her eyes, the kind that went deeper than just physical exhaustion. Dante stood as she entered, feeling an odd sense of relief just seeing her upright and moving.

"You look… better," he said, scanning her face, trying to gauge how she was really feeling.

Amy gave him a small, tired smile as she sat down beside him. "I may look better, but I still need food and rest." She glanced at the food on the table and reached for a piece of bread. "It feels strange," she admitted after a moment, "to be here… thousands of years in the past."

Dante nodded, chewing slowly as he watched her. "I know what you mean."

"Does this place even exist anymore? I mean, in our time?" she asked after a bite of meat.

He shrugged. "It's really a shame if it doesn't." He glanced around.

Amy took another bite of food, her eyes drifting around the room. He could tell her thoughts were elsewhere. He didn't push her to talk. They both needed this moment of peace, even if it was fleeting.

He wasn't naive enough to think this calm would last. There was too much ahead of them—too many dangers, too many unknowns. But for now, in this quiet room with Amy beside him, the world outside seemed distant. And for the first time in a long while, Dante allowed himself to feel the slightest bit of relief.

He was no longer alone.

Once they were both stuffed with food, they sat in some chairs with thick, soft cushions on them that surrounded a small round table.

"Prometheus said that if Pandora wakes, the world could end. I don't know if I believe him, but..."

"But what?" Amy asked, leaning back further into the cushions.

"If Prometheus doesn't want Pandora to wake, and Moros does," Dante finished, his voice barely above a whisper, "that means we have to stop him."

"He doesn't. Moros doesn't want Pandora around. From what I saw when I faced him, he was afraid of me. Her." She shook her head. "Pandora. He feared that she was already awake. Then, when I wavered, he..." She closed her eyes. "He shot me with a bolt of power, and I woke up just outside of town."

The weight of her words settled over him like a heavy cloak.

Pandora, Moros, the end of the world—it was all too much. And what was that bit about Pandora's box?

"Do you remember the myths? The Greek gods?" he asked her.

"Some of it. I wasn't that into history like you were. Names and some details. Like, I know about Pandora. How she was given a box and told to guard it." She yawned. "You? What do you remember?"

"Not much," he said, knowing she was too tired to continue the conversation. "There's a bed through there." He motioned towards the sheer curtains, beyond which sat a large bed.

"We can't just take over someone's home." She yawned again.

He chuckled. "Trust me, they think we're gods. Whoever lived here before has been relocated. At least for the night. It was the same in Thessalia."

"You were in Thessalia?" she asked, sitting up slightly.

He nodded. "Yeah, Brea sent me there. I was there for a few days before I came here. I just got here about two hours before you arrived."

She frowned. "Okay, so, where is here?"

"Delos Island. The best I can tell is around 600 to 800 BC."

"How can you tell?" She leaned her head back again. "It's not like they have a calendar or the internet to sync your clock to."

He chuckled. "No, but the boats in which they brought me to the island were a good clue. I remember seeing drawings of them in our history books. Like you said, I was somewhat of a history buff."

She smiled. "Did you ever think we'd end up here?" She motioned with her hands. "You look like a freaking gladiator. I look like..."

"A goddess," he finished for her, and he saw her smile waver. "No, if I'd believed for a moment we'd be in this position, I would have spent more time learning history than flirting with Lilly Thomas."

Amy laughed. "Lilly broke your heart."

"No." He frowned. "Just... bruised it. What about you and your latest..."

"Ryan?" she answered with a groan. "Heart was officially bruised, stabbed, sliced, diced, and left in a pile with the trash," she admitted.

"Ouch. That bad?" He winced.

She shrugged. "I'm over him now."

He wanted to say that was good but held back. Instead, he motioned to the bed. "Go, get some rest."

"What about you?" She glanced around. "I only see one bed."

He smiled. "Is that an invitation?"

She chuckled, standing up. "You know, for a guy who's from the future, you have some pretty outdated pickup lines."

He laughed while she disappeared through the drapes into the bedroom.

Dante shook his head, still smiling to himself as he moved over to the bigger sofa. The lighthearted moment eased some of the tension that had been building all day, but beneath the humor, he knew they were both dealing with the weight of what was to come. He stretched out on the sofa, listening to the soft sounds of the evening outside the window.

They were different than modern city noises and far more soothing. Exhaustion pulled at him, and before long, his eyes drifted shut.

Sometime later, a faint sound woke him. At first, he thought it was just the wind, but then he heard it again—a soft whimper, barely audible. His senses sharpened as he realized it was coming from the bedroom. He sat up, his heart pounding, and walked quietly towards the doorway.

Amy was thrashing in her sleep, her face contorted in

distress. Sweat glistened on her forehead as she mumbled, lost in the grip of whatever nightmare had her trapped.

"Amy…" Dante whispered softly, stepping closer to her bedside. He sat down gently beside her and reached out and touched her shoulder softly. "Amy, wake up."

She jerked awake with a start, gasping for breath. Her eyes were wide with fear as they locked onto his. For a moment, she seemed lost, her mind still tethered to whatever horror had plagued her dreams.

"Hey, it's okay," he said, his voice soothing as he pulled her closer to him in a soft hug. "It was just a dream."

Amy held him for a moment, then pulled back and wiped her damp face with trembling hands. "It wasn't just a dream. It was… it felt too real."

He watched her closely. "Want to tell me?"

She hesitated, her gaze distant. "Moros… he was everywhere. The darkness, his army… they destroyed everything. Everyone. Hope… she tried to fight, but… he killed her. I saw it. Over and over. I watched your sister die. My brother, my nephew, and my nieces. They all died." Her voice cracked, raw with the emotion she was barely holding back. "No matter what I did, I couldn't stop it. Everyone died."

Dante's chest tightened. Hearing Hope's name sent a sharp pang through him, but seeing Amy like this, torn apart by her visions of the future, was worse. He took a deep breath, trying to stay calm for her sake.

"You said you saw this all in the future?" Dante asked, his voice low.

Amy nodded her head, her hands fidgeting with the edge of the blanket. "It wasn't just a vision. It happened. Every time, somehow, it ends the same way. Moros is going to win."

Dante took her hand in his. "What you're seeing, from

The Stars

what you said, is one possible future. That doesn't mean it's set in stone."

"But what if it is?" she whispered, her voice barely audible.

He squeezed her hand gently. "Then we change it. We fight back, and we don't give up. We can still stop him."

Amy's eyes searched his, looking for hope, for reassurance, and Dante held her gaze, refusing to show any sign of doubt. He couldn't. Not now. Not when they were both on the edge of something so massive.

"I won't let Moros take everything from us. And I won't let him hurt you again," he continued softly.

Her lip quivered, and for a second, she looked like she might break. But instead, she nodded, her expression hardening with determination. "We'll stop him."

Dante smiled, though it didn't quite reach his eyes. "Damn right we will."

Amy exhaled slowly, the tension easing slightly from her body. "I'm sorry. I didn't mean to wake you by freaking out."

"You're allowed to freak out," Dante said easily. "We're in the middle of ancient Greece. We've both seen gods and talked to them. You even battled one," he pointed out.

She laughed lightly, a soft, tired sound. "Yeah, and everyone believes we're gods too." She sighed. "If I'm gonna have any more nightmares, maybe you should stick around."

Dante grinned. "You want me to stay here? Guard the door?"

"No," she said softly, reaching out to grab his arm before he could move away. "Stay here. With me."

He blinked, a little surprised, but nodded. Without a word, he lay back beside her, keeping a respectable distance but close enough that she could feel his presence.

As the quiet of the room settled over them, Amy's breathing slowly steadied. Dante stared up at the ceiling, his mind racing with the weight of her words. Moros. The future. The possibility of losing everything—again.

He wouldn't let it happen.

Not while he was still breathing.

And certainly not while Amy was by his side.

Chapter Eleven

When Amy woke, there was a heavy arm draped across her waist, pinning her to the soft mattress. For a moment, she forgot where, and most importantly, when she was.

She knew instantly that it was Dante beside her. The memory of him being there for her wasn't foggy at all—the quick looks he'd given her all last night, the flirting humor they'd shared between the darker topics.

He somehow made her heart flutter like no other had. Ever could.

She must have moved because his hand shifted.

"Sorry," he mumbled and started to pull away.

"No." She held him still. "It's okay." She sighed slightly. "Just... let's enjoy this for a moment."

His deep chuckle had her smiling. "I guess you didn't need any quick and witty pickup lines?"

She nudged his ribs with a finger. "Just because I like to be held doesn't mean sex is on the table."

He shifted slightly until he was looking down at her. God, he was gorgeous.

"But it's not officially *off* the table?" His eyebrows rose slightly.

As an answer, she lifted and brushed her lips against his. It wasn't their first kiss, but the awkward teenage peck they'd shared years before paled in comparison to the heat of his lips against hers now.

"My god," she moaned when he shifted closer.

"You gotta let me try that again," he said softly. "I need time to prepare for the kick of power your lips hold." With a grin, he lowered his head and brushed his lips against hers again.

This time, she relaxed into his touch and allowed him to take full control. Basically, she melted into his gentle hold of her. How could she not? He felt and tasted so good.

When his hands finally brushed her bare skin, little waves of pleasure pulsed through her.

Then he stilled.

"I... don't think we're alone," he whispered, and motioned towards the curtains.

She stilled and then heard movement in the next room. Embarrassment caused her cheeks to heat as Dante rolled off her.

She held her breath as they listened to the trays of food being replaced in the next room.

When the room was silent, Dante stood up and walked to pull the curtain aside.

"Fresh food," he said, looking back at her. "I'll let you dress." He pulled something into the room from the other room. "I'm sure they left this for you," he said, setting the yellow material down on a bench. "I'll change into whatever they brought me and meet you..." He nodded to the room.

"Dante?" She sat up, stopping him from leaving. "Where, um, how..."

The Stars

He frowned in confused, then laughed. "Bathroom is there." He motioned to a large bowl on the floor in the corner. "Sink." He pointed to another large bowl on a table. "Welcome to the dark ages." He chuckled as he walked out of the room.

Amy watched as Dante disappeared through the curtain, leaving her alone in the room. The yellow fabric he had set down on the bench seemed to glow faintly in the morning light. She sighed, running a hand through her hair as she swung her legs over the side of the bed.

As much as she appreciated the hospitality, the reality of her surroundings hit her again. This wasn't her world—not even close. The bowls that Dante pointed out to her didn't exactly scream comfort, but she had to make do.

After she relieved herself and washed up with some fragrant powder that she hoped was soap, she splashed her face with water from the "sink"—a term she used loosely.

Then she stood and approached the gown that had been left for her, running her fingers along its soft, almost silky texture. It was finely made, more luxurious than she had expected, especially considering the rough conditions. She held it up and smiled.

Amy dressed, enjoying the feeling of the cool fabric settling against her skin. The dress fit her perfectly.

Once she was ready, she pushed the curtain aside and stepped into the main room. Dante was already seated at the table, dressed in a simple tunic that looked far more regal on him than she expected. His eyes lifted as she entered, and for a second he seemed to forget how to speak.

"You look..." He cleared his throat, his eyes lingering on her. "Amazing."

She felt her cheeks blush, though she tried to hide it. "You clean up pretty well yourself."

They shared a small smile before she joined him at the table. Fresh food had been laid out: bread, cheese, some kind of roasted meat, and fruits that looked oddly familiar yet different at the same time. She realized just how hungry she was, her stomach rumbling as she reached for a piece of bread.

They ate in comfortable silence for a while, and then Dante finally spoke. "This place... it's starting to feel less like a dream and more like a reality I can't escape."

Amy chewed, nodding thoughtfully. "I know what you mean."

"Every time I think I've adjusted, something happens to remind me just how far we are from home."

"Home," she echoed.

"Feels like a distant memory."

Amy glanced at him, seeing a flicker of something in his eyes. Sadness? Longing? She wasn't sure. But she knew the feeling well. They had both been thrust into this world with no real choice and now they were trying to navigate it together.

Dante leaned back in his chair, stretching slightly before he spoke again. "I thought I'd miss modern conveniences more than I do," he said, picking at a piece of fruit. "But honestly, there's something about this place... like it's alive, watching us."

Amy felt a chill run down her spine at his words. "Yeah, I get that too. Like... we're being observed, every move we make."

"By the gods, no doubt," Dante said, his tone half-joking, half-serious. "We're not exactly off the radar."

Amy pushed her plate away, her appetite fading as the reality of their situation settled over her again. "So, what now?"

The Stars

Dante sighed, looking around the room. "I guess we wait. The town's leader seemed to think we'd know when it was time to move on. For now, we enjoy the comforts they've offered... even if it feels a little too good to be true."

Amy nodded, biting her lip as her mind wandered to Moros and the dark future she couldn't shake the memory of. "Do you ever feel like, no matter what we do, it's not going to be enough?"

Dante's eyes darkened, and he set down his drink. "Sometimes. But I refuse to believe that deep down. We've already come this far, and we're still standing." He reached out, placing his hand over hers on the table. "We'll figure this out."

She looked down at their hands, his warmth steadying her as she gave him a small, grateful smile.

Before they could say anything else, the door creaked open and the town's leader stepped inside, his face solemn but welcoming. "It's time," he said, gesturing for them to follow.

Amy and Dante exchanged a glance.

"Time?" Amy asked.

"The Fates await." He motioned towards the doors.

Moments later, they were helped into a very small rowboat with a young man working the oars.

They shoved off without any more words from the leader and watched as the island disappeared behind them.

The boat rocked gently as Amy gazed at the island ahead, surrounded by a veil of early morning mist.

The journey was a quiet one, with Dante sitting beside her. When they approached the smaller island, they spotted a dark silhouette of a temple resting atop a fog-covered hill. Large waves crashed against the wooden sides of the boat, despite the calm seas. Amy's nerves felt anything but steady.

"I guess that is where we're heading," Dante muttered, pointing towards the temple.

The building seemed to blend into the dark skies, a shadow against shadowy land.

Amy nodded, her heart thudding in her chest. She couldn't shake the feeling that whatever awaited them inside would change everything. As the boat neared the shore, the rower—a man of few words—brought them in close, letting them disembark onto the rocky beach. Without a word, he pushed off again, leaving them alone on the island.

"I guess that means there's no turning back," Dante said, his voice tight. He held out his hand and she eagerly put her hand in his.

They began the slow trek up the rocky hillside, the rough stone path winding beneath their feet. She'd never wished for a pair of sneakers as much as she did then. The simple leather sandals did little to protect her toes from the sharp rocks.

The wind whispered around them, carrying with it the sound of distant waves. As they climbed, she felt like something—or someone—was watching them. The temple loomed larger with each step, an ancient, imposing structure of crumbling stone and moss-covered pillars. How could this place be real?

When they reached the entrance, it was nothing but a gaping black maw. Cold air flowed from within, carrying the scent of something old and forgotten.

"Ready?" Dante asked, his hand squeezing hers, offering both reassurance and comfort.

The Stars

"As ready as I'll ever be," she replied as they stepped inside.

The darkness enveloped them instantly, their footsteps echoing across the stone floor. Amy's eyes struggled to adjust, but slowly, shapes began to take form. In the center of the chamber stood a large stone bowl, deep and wide, etched with intricate symbols. The bowl seemed to pulse with an energy, a presence that filled the room.

As they moved closer, a soft light flickered to life around the bowl. Then suddenly, three figures emerged from the dark shadows.

They were women—young, beautiful, with flowing gowns like the one she wore, only theirs shifted around them like mist. Each woman had long, ethereal hair, pale skin, and eyes that gleamed with knowledge far beyond human understanding.

The first woman stepped forward.

"I am Clotho, the Spinner," she said with a delicate smile on her lips as her fingers worked invisible threads in the air. "The thread of fate is not bound by time, not by choice."

The second stepped forward. "I am Lachesis, the Allotter." She moved next to the other woman, her gaze sharp, calculating, as if measuring them both. "Each life follows a path, one set long ago."

And the third moved forward. "I am Atropos, the Inflexible." She stood behind them both, her presence heavy, as though she could end the world with a mere flick of her fingers. Her face was stern, eyes piercing. "The end has already been written. You cannot change what must be."

Amy's breath caught in her throat as she suddenly realized who they were—the Fates, the sisters of destiny. Greek myths had been told for centuries about these women.

These... witches. No god, not even Zeus, could destroy them.

"What do you mean?" she asked, her voice wavering.

Clotho's hands continued to move, weaving threads only she could see. "Pandora has always awakened."

Lachesis's eyes flicked to Dante. "Epimetheus has always been the key to awakening Pandora."

Atropos stepped forward, her fingers trailing along the edge of the bowl. "The two of you will fulfill your roles. It is not a matter of if but when."

Dante took a step forward, his fists clenched. "What does that mean? What role? I don't even know what you're talking about."

The Fates turned their eyes on him, and as they did, something shifted. Their youthful features began to fade, wrinkles deepening, hair whitening. The air grew colder, as though time itself was unraveling in their presence.

"It has already begun," Lachesis whispered, her voice echoing through the chamber. "Pandora has always awakened and will always awaken. You cannot stop what has already happened," she repeated.

Amy's heart raced. "But we've come to stop it—to stop Moros."

The three crones cackled and then said together.

"Only Elpis can stop Moros," Clotho whispered.

She thought Pandora was the key to stopping Moros. From Mia's vision, she knew who Elpis was. Not that she remembered much of what she'd seen. Maybe that was the "sleep" she was supposed to wake from?

"I thought Pandora was supposed to stop Moros?" Dante asked.

"Elpis and Pandora together, as never before," Clotho added.

The Stars

"How do we find Elpis?" Dante asked.

"Pandora will waken Elpis when it is time," Lachesis answered.

"How do we control Pandora?" Dante asked. "Isn't she the one who can destroy everything?"

Clotho shook her head gently, her eyes sorrowful. "Pandora is beyond your control. The forces that bind her are older than the gods themselves. You cannot change what has already been written in the threads of fate."

Atropos stepped closer to them, her once beautiful face now a mask of age and finality. "The threads have woven themselves around you both. Epimetheus must wake Pandora from her slumber. Pandora must help Elpis. It is your destiny."

Dante's jaw clenched as he turned to Amy, his voice tight with frustration. "I'm not Epimetheus."

"You are who you've always been," Lachesis said softly. "Just as she is Pandora."

"How?" Dante asked, sounding defeated.

"You know," Atropos said, touching the hollow spot above her own heart.

Amy gasped, the weight of their words sinking in. "I'm not Pandora. I'm just... Amy."

The Fates exchanged knowing glances, their forms now ancient, crumbling like statues eroded by time. Clotho spoke last, her voice barely a whisper. "You will remain here, bound to this time, until your fates are fulfilled. There is no escape."

The words sent a chill down Amy's spine. She glanced at Dante, his expression hardening as the truth settled in.

Destiny had brought them here, and destiny would see them through. Whether they liked it or not.

Chapter Twelve

This time, when they returned to Delos, they were guided to what appeared to be a temple not far from the theater at the base of the mountain. The building overlooked the small town on one side and a rocky overlook to the sea on the other. It was set apart from all the other buildings.

"You are to remain here," the leader said and, without waiting for a response, he turned and left quickly.

Dante watched the leader walk away, his pace quickening with every step as though he couldn't wait to put distance between them. The man hadn't even looked them in the eyes. It was like they carried a curse no one wanted to be around now.

"At first, he seemed to be helping us," Dante muttered, his eyes scanning the empty path ahead. "Now I think he's afraid of us." His voice held a bitter edge. He glanced back at Amy, who stood silently beside him, her arms wrapped around her body as if she could protect herself from the weight of everything they had learned.

The temple loomed behind them as the leader disappeared down the pathway, a grand structure compared to the simplicity of the Fates' island, yet it carried a heavy silence, almost sacred. Dante pushed open the large wooden door, and they stepped inside. The air was thick and musty, and the only sound was their footsteps echoing across the stone floor. It was bare, except for a few pieces of old furniture—benches and a large table in the center of the room, a small bed in the room towards the back.

There was no welcome, no conversation, just a sense of isolation.

"Home sweet home, I guess," he said dryly. "I guess they're serious about keeping us here," he added with a slight laugh as he ran a hand through his hair.

Amy didn't respond, just sat down on a wooden chair in the corner. The silence between them stretched, heavy with unspoken worries. A knock at the door broke through the tension, but when Dante opened it, no one stood outside—just trays of food that had been left on the doorstep. He glanced around, but whoever had delivered the meal had quickly gone.

"Guess we're not exactly welcome dinner guests," he said, lifting the trays and carrying them to the table. "Not even a hello. They're treating us like outcasts now."

Amy sat down across from him, her eyes distant. "Maybe that's what we are now." She picked at the bread in front of her, not really eating, just tearing pieces off and setting them aside. "The Fates said we're destined for this. That we can't stop it."

Dante leaned back in his chair, staring at the ceiling for a moment before closing his eyes. He hadn't been able to shake the image of the Fates from his mind—the way they had appeared young and ethereal, only to age with each word they spoke. It was like each word represented the weight of time itself.

When the sun began to set, painting the sky in streaks of red and orange, they moved outside onto the small stone balcony that overlooked the sea. The air was warm and soothing.

"At least our jail has a beautiful setting," she said softly with a sigh. "I've never seen such a colorful sunset before."

He nodded in agreement as he settled into one of the old wooden chairs, his gaze fixed on the horizon. He could feel Amy's presence beside him, quiet, contemplative. It had been hours since they returned from the Fates' temple, and still, their words echoed in his mind.

"You okay?" he asked softly, glancing sideways at her.

She leaned forward, her elbows resting on her knees as she stared at the dark waves far below them. "I don't know," she admitted after a long pause. "It feels like no matter what we do, we're just... stuck. Like everything is out of our hands."

"Fate," Dante said sarcastically, the frustration simmering beneath his calm exterior. "Yeah, I get that. It's like they already have everything planned out. We're just the pieces moving along the gods' damn game board."

Amy looked at him then, her eyes searching his. "What if they're right? What if this is supposed to happen—Pandora waking, Moros... all of it?"

Dante clenched his jaw, the thought of it twisting like a knife in his chest. "I'm not ready to accept that. I can't just... sit here and let it happen. There has to be something we can do."

"They said it's already happened," Amy reminded him, her voice soft but insistent. "That it always happens, no matter what."

He exhaled slowly, running a hand over his face. "Maybe. But I can't believe that our only purpose is to be pawns in some ancient prophecy. We're not just here to watch everything burn. There has to be another way."

Amy shifted, her gaze turning back to the sea. "I hope you're right. But what if the Fates are right, and we can't stop it? What if no matter what we do, it's already set in stone?" She was silent for a moment. "What if... waking Pandora means the end of everything that makes me, me?"

He reached over and took her hand in his. "I'll do everything in my power not to let that happen."

She sighed. "You're supposed to already be Epimetheus. Do you feel any different?"

He shook his head. "No."

"They didn't say Epimetheus had to wake, so that means you're already him. Which means, you're still you."

He nodded and agreed with her. "So maybe it's just as simple as believing you're Pandora?" he wondered out loud.

"I don't think so. They mentioned that Epimetheus had to wake Pandora." She glanced at him.

"I don't care what the Fates said," he said finally, his voice low but determined. "We make our own choices."

Amy smiled faintly, though it didn't quite reach her eyes. "You're stubborn."

"Damn right," he said, his lips twitching into a grin. "And I plan on fighting this thing until there's no fight left."

"What if..."—she bit her bottom lip, sucked it into her mouth—"we're supposed to..."

"There you go again, bringing up sex," he joked when she didn't finish her obvious thought.

"Whatever." She threw her hands up in frustration and stood against the railing. "What do you want with us?" she screamed into the night air.

He chuckled and stood beside her. "Well, from all the tales, the gods did sleep around a lot. Right?"

He placed a hand on her shoulder. "It's not like we haven't been dancing around it for years."

"Years?" she teased as she looked up at him.

"For me, yes, years," he admitted, running his eyes over her face. The moonlight made her soft skin glow. She was a goddess. The most beautiful woman he'd ever seen. There was no doubt of that.

"Okay, years," she admitted as she moved slightly closer to him. "After prom, you... never called." She tilted her head slightly.

"Things got... complicated."

"Right." She nodded. "Laura Stein complicated," she said with a slight frown.

He rolled his eyes. "She was a distraction from the scary feelings I had about you."

Her eyebrows rose slightly. "That is the lamest excuse for dumping a girl that I've ever heard."

He chuckled and pulled her closer. "We're here now. I guess that means we weren't fated to be together until now."

She softened against him. Her hands went to his shoulders. "Three thousand years give or take. I guess it was bound to happen sometime," she whispered just before their lips met.

There had been a few times in his life when he'd felt his mind, body, and heart were out of control. The moment Amy's mouth touched his, he lost every single sliver he'd ever had. His body, his desires, and his feelings for her consumed his every heartbeat.

His body stilled as she ran her hands over his arms slowly until her fingers lay flat over his chest.

"Dante," she whispered. "I don't know what's happening here but tell me you feel it too."

He nodded, unable to voice just what he felt. His fingers were firmly gripping the golden dress she wore. He was afraid that if he touched her, his very essence would explode.

"Dante, touch me," she said after the kiss deepened.

"If I do... what will happen?" he asked as her lips trailed over his neck. Then she stilled.

"I'm still me," she whispered, leaning back to look deep into his eyes. "You're Dante, I'm Amy. That's all I know."

He sighed and rested his forehead against hers.

"Neither of us can promise that," he said softly, pulling back. "If I touch you, there won't be any going back for me."

Her hand came up slowly and cupped his face.

"For either of us. There's no going back no matter what we do," she said as their eyes locked.

The sadness in her eyes almost overtook him. The pain, the sorrow of what she'd witnessed in the future. The loss she'd experienced had brought an empty look to her eyes. That look was gone when she looked at him.

"Whatever the future holds, right now, we're here. Together." She smiled slightly. "That's enough for me." She lifted on her toes and brushed her lips across his. "Let that be enough for tonight."

Feeling her body vibrate against his, he was at a complete loss. Without a word, he gently lifted her in his arms and carried her inside. When he laid her on the bed, he realized that from the moment he'd seen her again, the moment she'd come back into his life, he'd lost his heart to her.

Maybe it had never really belonged to him and had been hers all along.

Her slight smile took away the last of his strength. When he covered her body, everything he had been before melted into one thing. One goal. To protect her from whatever came next.

This time, he didn't hold back when he kissed her. His hands roamed over her body, pushing, pulling the soft material up, away, until the soft skin of her silky leg was under his fingertips.

Her nails scraped against his exposed skin. When she released a soft chuckle, he stilled.

"How do you remove this thing?" she asked, tugging on his clothes.

He smiled and in one quick swipe he had the tunic falling away.

"You're going to have to teach me how to do that." She smiled up at him. "I like this getup almost as much as your cop uniform. Sexy." She wiggled her eyebrows.

"Later," he promised and covered her body with his, settling between her thighs as she wrapped her legs around his hips. Only a thin sliver of silk separated them.

"You kept these?" he asked, running his fingers across her silk panties.

She smiled. "The last little connection to the future. Besides, I'd just purchased them."

He chuckled as he slid a fingertip over them, making her breath catch.

"I have no idea what they did with the rest of my clothes." She sighed. "You?"

He shrugged. "I hadn't thought about it."

"Dante," she whispered as she arched for him and he trailed his mouth over her shoulder.

"Tell me what you want," he said, watching her skin flush for him. "This?" he asked, and slid his finger underneath the silk to touch her. She bit her bottom lip and nodded. "More?" he asked and she nodded again.

He removed his fingers and her eyes opened. He smiled. "Tell me."

"I... want you to touch me," she whispered. "To kiss me."

"Don't be shy now," he warned with a grin.

She smiled. "Dante, touch me. Slide your fingers in me, your tongue in me. Play with my clit. Fill me." She took his wrist in her hand and pulled it back towards her. He did what she asked, gliding his fingertips over the silk until she was wet and panting, demanding him. Then he dipped down and placed his mouth over the silk. When he no longer could go without tasting her, he ripped it aside.

He didn't know how much longer he could control himself. Feeling her slickness, smelling her sweet scent of arousal, tasting her skin.

When he nudged her legs further apart so he could run his eyes over her in the moonlight, he realized just how much he'd wanted her all these years. How he'd dreamed of this very moment.

Destiny.

The three Fates had talked of this. How this moment had always been. They had been locked to this time and place. To each other.

When he slipped inside her, power surged deep in his chest, something he'd never felt before. It vibrated and warmed him from the core.

Yes. He was who he had always been. Would always be. Hers.

Chapter Thirteen

Once again, Dante's arm was pinning her to the bed. He shifted slightly in his sleep, his arm heavy across her waist, holding her close. The warmth of the morning sunbathed them in a soft golden light, filtering through the open balcony doors and casting long shadows across the stone floor. For a moment, Amy just lay there, feeling the steady rise and fall of his chest against her back, the soft rustle of the sea breeze stirring the curtains, the distant sound of waves crashing against the shore.

This world was so still. So peaceful. So... wild.

This was where she wanted to stay. For as long as she could. It was pure heaven.

Her mind drifted back to the night before, the intensity of it all—how they'd fallen into each other, finding solace in the chaos, the uncertainty of what lay ahead.

In this quiet moment, it felt as though time had slowed, the world outside their door forgotten, and all that existed was this—Dante beside her, their bodies entwined, and the gentle peace of the new day.

Nothing inside her had changed or awakened. She was still Amy. Just Amy. No Pandora. No threats to the world around them or the world that was to come.

She felt him stir again, a soft murmur escaping his lips as he buried his face into the curve of her neck, his breath warm against her skin. A smile tugged at her lips, and for a brief moment, she allowed herself to forget the weight of the prophecy, the Fates, and everything that loomed ahead of them.

Dante's fingers flexed, his grip tightening slightly.

"Mornin'," he mumbled, his voice deep and rough.

Amy shifted beneath him, turning slightly so she could look at him. "Morning."

He lifted his head slightly, squinting against the sunlight pouring in through the open balcony as he blinked awake, his eyes still clouded with sleep. He stretched, his muscles rippling under his skin as he finally released her from his hold, though his hand lingered on her waist, his touch lazy and familiar. "You're warm," he muttered, half-asleep still, his lips grazing her shoulder.

"You too," she teased softly, running her fingers through his hair.

For a moment, they just lay there, the quiet between them comfortable. But as the warmth of the sun grew and the world outside began to wake, reality started to creep back in. The temple. The Fates. The inescapable truth of what awaited them.

Dante let out a slow breath and finally rolled onto his back, staring up at the ceiling as if it held answers. His voice was softer when he spoke again. "Last night... we talked about fighting back, about not letting them control us."

Amy nodded, her heart tightening at the thought. "Do you still believe we can?"

The Stars

His eyes shifted towards her, his gaze unwavering. "I do. I have to. I don't care what they said—we're not just pieces on their board. We're not powerless." He glanced over at her. "Do you feel different?"

She shook her head. "You?"

He shook his head.

She studied him for a moment.

"I'm not sure what I believe," she whispered, moving closer, pressing a soft kiss to his lips. "For now, all that matters to me is this." She kissed him again as his hands moved to her hips, slowly moving up and down her skin.

The passion she felt vibrating between them was something she'd never experienced before. It caused her body to heat to almost a breaking point. This time, when he slid inside her, twin moans echoed in the room, and she was pretty sure the entire world shifted around them.

Time and place no longer mattered to them. Exploring one another was the sole focus of the rest of their lives.

Once they were both breathless and she lay across his chest, it suddenly dawned on her. She had always felt this way about Dante.

How long had they flirted with one another? When had the attraction between them started?

Middle school? Earlier?

The first time she could remember thinking of him as more than a friend was when he'd stood up for her against a couple of bullies in gym class.

She'd been the awkward skinny and too-tall girl with no boobs or hips to speak of. As the only girl taller than every single boy in her class back then, she'd been an easy target. A few years later, none of that would matter when her boobs came in and all the boys in the class towered over her five-foot-seven frame after she stopped growing upward.

Dante had been the only one, besides her brother, to defend her. From that moment on, she'd looked at him differently. Then they'd gone to the dance together and had shared their first brief kiss. Every man she'd dated after had paled in comparison.

"How long do you think this will go on?" he asked as their skin cooled.

She didn't want to answer because she didn't want her time with him to end, here, where the entire world moved more slowly and, most importantly, wasn't on the verge of being destroyed.

When she didn't answer, he rolled over until she was pinned under him. "Amy?" He frowned as his eyes ran over her. "As much as I'm enjoying this, we have to get back."

"Do we?" she asked, her voice a little sharp. "Why?"

He blinked a few times. "I can give you a million reasons why." He brushed a strand of her hair away from her forehead. "Modern reasons..."

Amy stared up at him, her chest tight as she tried to find the words. His frown deepened, concern flickering in his eyes as his fingers lingered on her cheek.

"Modern reasons?" she whispered, trying to keep her voice steady. "What could be so important back there? You said it yourself—the Fates have their plans. They've already woven our threads. Maybe we can't change anything."

His hand stilled, his brow furrowing as he searched her face. "We're not just puppets, Amy. We've talked about that."

She closed her eyes, taking a slow breath. "But what if... what if I don't want to go back?" The confession felt heavy, like a weight finally lifting off her chest. "Here... with you... it's like none of it matters. Like the future isn't this... inevitable disaster."

The Stars

Dante's grip on her tightened, his body tensing above hers. "Amy, we can't just hide here forever. As much as I'd like to."

She met his gaze, her heart pounding in her chest. "But what if it's the only place where we can be together? Where we're safe?"

Dante's expression softened, and for a moment, she saw the same conflict mirrored in his eyes. He leaned down, pressing his forehead to hers. "I get it," he whispered. "Believe me, I do. But we have to face it. Whatever the Fates have planned for us, we can't let it happen without a fight."

Her throat tightened, the reality of it settling in. The future she'd seen... Moros. Death. The destruction of everything. She felt it every time she closed her eyes, the nightmares gnawing at the edges of her mind.

Dante kissed her gently, his lips lingering on hers as if trying to reassure her. "We'll make every moment count, starting with right now. But we can't give up. Not yet."

She swallowed hard, blinking back the tears that threatened to spill. In the safety of this moment, in the warmth of the morning light, it was easy to pretend that none of it mattered. That the end wasn't coming for them. But deep down, she knew he was right. They couldn't escape forever.

"Okay," she breathed, her voice barely a whisper. "But... can we just stay here a little longer?"

Dante smiled softly, his hand brushing over her cheek, gentle and reassuring. "Yeah," he murmured, pressing another kiss to her lips. "Besides, we still need to figure out just how in the hell we get out of here."

She smiled up at him. "How about a walk?"

He nodded. "Food first." He glanced around. "Do you think they're going to deliver food to us up here?"

She shrugged. "It does seem like we're being ostracized. Separated from the town for a reason. Maybe punished?" she continued as he rolled away and they sat up to dress.

"Punished? For what? We didn't even do anything—at least not yet," he said.

"Maybe that's the point. Or they're worried we will," she suggested.

Amy pulled her gown over her shoulders, tying the sash as she glanced at Dante. He was struggling with his shirt, and the familiar sight of him doing something so ordinary brought a brief flicker of warmth to her chest. But her mind kept spinning. She couldn't shake the feeling that they were being watched and scrutinized. Separated. It wasn't just paranoia—it was something deeper. The way the villagers had avoided them, the way they were being kept here, isolated, it all felt... intentional.

As Dante finished dressing, he walked to the balcony, his eyes fixed on the sea. Amy followed, leaning against the stone railing next to him. The fresh breeze off the water tickled her skin, but the beauty of the view couldn't distract her from the weight pressing on her chest.

"So what's the plan? We just wait here, in this time, until they decide to let us go?" he asked.

Amy wrapped her arms around herself, staring out over the endless horizon. "I don't think we have a choice. The Fates said this is where we need to be." She paused, the memory of those cryptic words tugging at her thoughts. "But that doesn't mean we can't find answers ourselves."

Dante's jaw tightened as he nodded, the frustration evident in the tense set of his shoulders. Amy understood—neither of them was the type to sit back and do nothing. But what were they supposed to do here, in this temple, cut off from the world?

The Stars

The knock on the door startled her. Amy exchanged a glance with Dante before turning towards the sound. A servant entered, silently holding a tray with bread, fruit, and water. He didn't speak, didn't even lift his head to look at them, just bowed slightly and left.

"Well," Dante muttered, "that answers the food question."

Amy walked over and grabbed a piece of bread from the tray. "Looks like."

He let out a dry laugh. "Great. Food and isolation. The perfect combo."

As they ate, they chatted about everything they could remember about the Fates, Greek myths, and the geography of the area.

The Fates' words kept replaying in her mind, looping endlessly. The inevitability of Pandora's awakening, the way they were destined to be here, fulfilling some ancient prophecy—none of it sat well with her.

Once they were done with their meal, Amy's eyes met his. "Okay, we have to figure out how to change the future." Amy's heart raced as the idea took root. "Theo," she said after a moment, the name sparking a glimmer of hope in the haze of uncertainty.

Dante's brow furrowed, his deep eyes searching hers. "Who is Theo?"

"The boy who brought me to you, remember?" she said, a small smile forming at the edges of her lips. "He didn't seem afraid of me, and kids... they tend to see things differently. Maybe he didn't get the memo to stay away from us."

Dante's frown softened as realization dawned. "You think we can find him?"

She nodded, feeling a rush of confidence. "I bet we can. He wasn't afraid, Dante. He seemed curious, if anything. And maybe, just maybe, he can help us figure out what's going on here. It's a long shot, but it's better than sitting here waiting for the Fates to decide everything."

Dante ran a hand through his hair, sighing. "Okay, so we get that walk in."

Amy's smile widened, and she felt a renewed sense of purpose. The sun was already high in the sky, warming everything around them, but there was plenty of time. They could try. She grabbed her sandals and slipped them on quickly, the urge to move, to do something, propelling her forward.

Dante followed her to the door, and together they stepped out into the midmorning air. It felt different now—less oppressive. The weight of the day still lingered, but with a new goal in mind, the world around them didn't seem quite as confining.

The narrow streets of the town were quiet, save for the occasional clatter of pottery or distant murmur of conversation. Amy led the way, her eyes scanning for any sign of Theo. She remembered how quickly he'd appeared before, like he had been waiting for her, like he knew something that she didn't.

Dante walked beside her, his hand brushing against hers as they moved through the village. The buildings blocked out the sunlight, casting long cool shadows. If they could find Theo, if they could get him to talk, maybe they'd finally get the answers they needed.

After a few minutes, Dante broke the silence. "Do you think this kid knows more than he let on?"

Amy shrugged, her eyes still scanning. "Maybe. He brought me to you like he knew exactly where I was supposed to be. That can't be a coincidence."

The Stars

Dante hummed in agreement, his fingers brushing her arm lightly. "Let's hope we find him, then."

They finished going through the main part of town and then she had an idea. She turned and they made their way towards the outskirts.

They found Theo just outside of town in a field, tending to his goats. He was perched on a rock, calmly watching over his small herd as they grazed on the patches of grass. As Amy and Dante approached, Theo looked up, a small smile playing on his lips.

"Found you," Amy said, her smile tugging at her lips.

Theo grinned. "I wasn't hiding."

Dante chuckled softly beside her. "Smart kid."

Theo stood up, dusting his hands on his clothes.

"What do you want?" he asked, though there was no suspicion in his tone. He was curious, just like before.

"We need to know if there's somewhere else where we can learn more," Amy said, glancing at Dante. "You know, like a place where the gods talk to people?"

Theo thought about it for a moment before his eyes lit up. "There is!" he said, excitement flashing across his face. "High up on the mountain. There's a place where the gods talk to man."

Amy felt a flicker of hope. Maybe this was it—the place that could give them more answers. "Do you know how to get there?"

Theo nodded. "You can't miss it. You just have to follow the trail that starts at the edge of town. It's almost a day's walk though."

Amy exchanged a glance with Dante. They were getting somewhere. "We'll go tomorrow," she said, already planning out the next day in her head. But then Theo's voice cut through her thoughts.

"Can I see your magic box again?" he asked. "I've been thinking about it."

Amy blinked in confusion before realizing what he meant. She pulled her phone out of her pocket, unlocked it, and showed him the screen. Her battery was close to being gone so she reminded herself to turn it off when they were done.

The boy's eyes lit up with fascination as she swiped through the photos, his small fingers tracing the light on the glass screen.

"It's not magic," she said with a smile, showing him a picture of the sea. "But I guess it might seem like it."

Theo's wide eyes darted between the images. "It shows the world, though. Like it's all inside there. The good. The bad."

Dante chuckled beside her. "Pretty much."

As Amy swiped through a few more photos, Dante leaned in close. "So, we head up to the mountain tomorrow?"

She nodded, her eyes still on Theo. "Yeah. It sounds like our best shot."

Theo handed the phone back to her, still staring at it like it was the most amazing thing he'd ever seen. "You should go soon," he said, his voice turning a little more serious. "Before it's too late. I'm told you must return to the temple each night and remain there until it's time."

Amy raised an eyebrow at that, but before she could ask what he meant, Theo smiled again and turned back to his goats.

"Well, thanks for the tip, kid," Dante said with a nod as they turned to leave.

"Good eve, Pandora, Epimetheus," he called over his shoulder.

Amy froze for a heartbeat. Then she turned to Dante. Dante's brow furrowed as he looked towards Theo. The kid had already disappeared behind the hillside.

Pandora and Epimetheus.

Amy's stomach twisted, the implications of the names sinking in.

Dante met her gaze, his expression a mirror of her shock. "Even he thinks that's our names."

"Then maybe the myths were never just stories—they were about us all along," she whispered.

Chapter Fourteen

The next morning, Dante woke up early just as the cool morning air slipped through the open windows, carrying the scent of wildflowers from the mountain. He lay still for a moment, his arm wrapped around Amy as her body warmed his.

"Today's the day," he murmured, more to himself than her, though Amy stirred slightly. She didn't fully wake, so he kissed the top of her head before slipping out of bed and stretching. His muscles ached from the tension coiling inside him. Today, he hoped, would bring them some answers.

By the time the sun had fully risen, they were on their way, following the old path Theo had mentioned. It wound steeply up the mountainside. The pathway cut through the wild brush, its dusty surface littered with small stones that crunched beneath their boots. The morning air was crisp at first, but as the sun climbed higher in the sky, it grew hotter and more intense.

The view of the village and sea below expanded and changed the higher they went. The ancient path felt almost untouched, forgotten by time, as if very few people had ever passed this way.

They had packed some of the fruit and cheese from breakfast into a bag to take with them, and they stopped for lunch and a drink of water at what appeared to be the halfway mark. At least she hoped they were halfway.

When they had walked for another two hours, she caught herself from falling and grew frustrated.

"How much farther, do you think?" Amy asked, her voice breathless but steady.

Dante wiped the sweat from his brow and looked ahead. "Not much, I hope." He could see a clearing ahead and could sense an almost magnetic pull. "We're getting close."

"I miss my tennis shoes," she said when he helped her over a fallen tree trunk.

He chuckled. "I miss coffee."

She groaned. "The tea they give us is close. But I could go for a Frappuccino right about now."

They rounded a bend, and there it was—an old, weather-beaten temple nestled against the side of the mountain. Its stone pillars were cracked and crumbling, moss creeping up the sides, but it was still standing. An air of ancient power surrounded it, pressing against Dante's skin, making the hair on his arms stand up.

"How long do you think this has been here?" she whispered

"Hundreds, maybe thousands of years."

Amy stepped up beside him, her eyes wide. "It's... beautiful, in a way."

They walked through the stone archway entrance, and the long shadows immediately cooled their skin. Inside, however, the air was still, thick with dust and the scent of time long forgotten. The chamber was huge, and the ceiling was arched. There were faded murals along the walls—scenes of battles, gods, and figures that felt eerily familiar.

At the far end of the building sat an altar.

"Do you think they used to sacrifice things there?" she asked, and he felt her shiver.

"Most likely. Look at the writing." He moved closer.

Above the altar, carved deep into the stone, were pictures and ancient writings. His eyes immediately focused on the words, and despite their age, he was surprised that he could read them clearly, as though the text had been waiting for him.

"The time will come when Pandora awakens, guided by Epimetheus. From the future they return, souls reborn, destined to battle gods and save all worlds."

He read the words aloud, his voice echoing through the empty chamber. Amy stepped closer, her breath hitching as she traced the carvings with her fingertips.

"It's our story," she whispered. "It's all right here. The two of us meet the djinn, Mia. Us, fighting the gods over and over." She motioned to the walls and, when he focused, he could see the many scenes of battle etched in the stones, though they were faded and covered with vines. The murals told the same tale thousands of times.

"Reincarnations. We've been here before. We've fought many times before," he said as his eyes scanned the images.

One mural showed a man and woman—him and Amy, he realized with a shock—standing before the gods, weapons in hand. Another depicted a massive battle, the two of them at the center, circled by almost a dozen others who fought beside them.

"This is what we're supposed to do," he muttered. "Fight the gods. Save... everything." His throat tightened at the thought of the monumental task ahead. They had been destined for this all along, even when they didn't know it. Dante clenched his fists. "I'm not afraid to fight. But how do we change the outcome? The answer to that has to be here."

Amy's hand slid into his, her grip firm and steady. "The answer is here somewhere," she said, her voice filled with a conviction that calmed him. "We've come this far. We've been through too much to fail now."

They stood there together, absorbing the enormity of it all, as the mountain winds whispered around them.

The air in the temple shifted around them suddenly. Instantly, they both sensed that there was a presence nearby. Dante felt a tingling in his skin, an electric charge that made the hairs on the back of his neck rise. He glanced at Amy and saw her eyes dart around the room, searching the shadows for something they couldn't yet see.

Then a figure stepped from behind the altar, tall and imposing. His features were sharp, carved with an otherworldly intensity, his eyes glowing with ancient wisdom and fury.

Prometheus.

The Titan who had defied Zeus to give fire to humanity. Prometheus's gaze settled on them, his lips curling into a knowing smirk.

"So you've found your temple, together again," he said, his voice deep, echoing through the temple. "Pandora and Epimetheus, reborn."

Amy gripped Dante's arm, her knuckles turning slightly white. Dante's muscles tensed, ready for whatever was coming next. The last time he'd had an encounter with Prometheus, he'd been warned. This time, he sensed that this wasn't going to be a friendly reunion.

"We're here to understand," Amy said her voice steady

The Stars

despite the fear flickering in her eyes. "To figure out our path."

Prometheus tilted his head, studying her, his expression unreadable. "Your path?" he repeated, almost mockingly. "Your path has already been written. You come here, again and again, always seeking answers, and always trying to change what cannot be changed."

His gaze darkened, and he took a step closer, his towering presence growing more menacing. "And you, Pandora"—he spat the name like a curse—"you seek to awaken that which should remain buried."

"Why must it remain buried?" Amy's breath hitched. "We're trying to stop this. To stop the gods from—"

"From what?" Prometheus interrupted, his voice rising with anger. "From the inevitable? You were given the gift of foresight, Epimetheus, but you always arrive too late. Always too late to prevent the destruction that *you* cause."

Dante clenched his fists, his pulse racing. "We're trying to fix this!" he snapped, stepping in front of Amy, shielding her from Prometheus's growing rage.

The Titan's eyes flashed dangerously. "You think you can fix what the gods have decreed? That you can stop what has already been set in motion?" He turned his gaze to Amy, and his expression twisted into something darker. "Pandora is the key to all worlds demise. She must not awaken."

Before Dante could react, Prometheus's body was engulfed in a bright yellow light and he lunged towards Amy, his hand outstretched as if to strike her down.

A primal fury ignited in Dante's chest, hotter and more powerful than anything he had ever felt. He moved without thinking, his body surging forward with strength he didn't know he possessed. His hand caught Prometheus's arm mid-swing, stopping the Titan in his tracks.

Prometheus's eyes widened, surprise flashing across his face as he stared down at Dante. "You..."

Dante didn't relent. He shoved Prometheus back with a force that sent him stumbling, his power shocking him for a moment. His heart pounded in his chest, his muscles burning with the raw strength coursing through him. His entire body was engulfed with a hot blue light that pulsed from his core.

Prometheus straightened, and for the first time a slow smile spread across his face, cold and calculating. "Ah, there you are, brother."

Dante's breath caught. The way Prometheus said the word *brother* suddenly caused his mind to wake to a memory he hadn't realized he carried. He wasn't just Epimetheus reborn. He was something more, something ancient, connected to the Titan before him in ways he couldn't yet fully understand.

They were... friends. Brothers.

Prometheus chuckled darkly, his gaze shifting between Dante and Amy. "Welcome back, Epimetheus. You always did have a penchant for protecting her. But the question remains... how long will you last this time?"

Dante's hands clenched into fists, every instinct screaming at him to strike again, to keep Amy safe at all costs. But Prometheus turned away, his smile fading as he looked towards the temple's entrance, the weight of centuries heavy in his posture.

"I grow tired of these games. You'll learn soon enough," Prometheus muttered, his voice lower, almost regretful. "This battle is not yours to win. It never was. This is why I gave the world Elpis." His eyes turned to Amy. "She is yours to find. But she too requires a catalyst. Find me in my

The Stars

future to wake her if you want to win this war once and for all. We are your missing pieces."

And with that, he disappeared, fading into the shadows as quickly as he had appeared, leaving Dante and Amy standing in the ancient temple alone.

Dante's fists unclenched slowly, the strength that had surged through him fading, leaving him feeling both powerful and vulnerable all at once. He turned to Amy, whose wide eyes met his, the shock still lingering between them.

"I guess we found our secret weapon," Amy said with a sigh.

"Did you feel that?" Dante asked, his voice thick with disbelief.

Amy turned to him and nodded, her breath shaky. "You... you glowed and you stopped him. Like a god."

Dante's mind raced, the words *Welcome back, brother* echoing in his mind. He swallowed hard, trying to piece together the fragments of his past life, of their shared destiny.

"Funny thing, I think we're friends," Dante said, his voice low.

Amy stepped closer, her hand finding him, her grip warm and firm. "Do you think you can control it? The power?"

He stepped back and thought about protecting Amy. Instantly, his body and his power reacted.

"Cool." She smiled at him. "Does it hurt?" She reached out and gently touched his glowing skin.

"No, just... it's different. I feel..." He flexed his arms. "Powerful."

After the adrenaline from the encounter with Prometheus

subsided, they sat together near the entrance of the temple, unpacking the rest of the food they'd brought with them and eating before they started the long journey back down.

Neither spoke much as their minds lingered on the revelations of the day. The ancient writings in the temple, Prometheus's appearance, Dante's newfound powers—it was all too much to process at once.

After they finished eating, Amy used the rest of her phone's battery to snap as many photos and videos of the temple walls as she could until it finally died.

Then the two of them began the descent down the mountain just as the air grew cooler, signaling that twilight was setting in. Amy walked close to him, their fingers brushing as they navigated the uneven path.

They had just reached the town as the colors in the sky deepened into purples and blues. When they returned to the secluded building they'd been staying in, the heaviness in the air hadn't lifted. The silence was almost suffocating, and even though the night had settled, it was obvious that Amy's unease hadn't faded.

"What's going on in your mind?" he asked as they stood out on the balcony.

"You said that Prometheus warned you not to wake me." He nodded in agreement. "Then, was that a lie? Why is he afraid of me?"

"Maybe he's like us, afraid of the future. He does want us to find him, which means he could be as trapped in fate as we are," he suggested.

"He did say he was tired of the game," she pointed out and he saw her relax. "That makes sense."

"I think we should rest," Dante finally said, though his tone carried a question more than a suggestion.

Amy nodded wordlessly.

The Stars

Later, as they lay in bed, the quiet of the night seemed to amplify the storm raging inside Amy. Dante noticed her tossing and turning, her breathing coming faster, more ragged. He reached out, his hand brushing against her arm.

"Amy?" he whispered.

Her eyes fluttered open for a second before squeezing shut again. She was still asleep, caught in the throes of some nightmare. Her face twisted, her lips parted as if trying to scream, but no sound came out.

"Amy," Dante said again, louder this time.

Suddenly, she gasped, sitting up with a start. Her wide eyes darted around the room, searching for something, her chest rising and falling rapidly as if she couldn't catch her breath.

"Hey, it's okay. It was just a dream," he said, sitting up beside her.

She turned to him, her eyes glassy with unshed tears. "It wasn't just a dream," she whispered, her voice shaking. "It was real. I saw him again."

Dante frowned, his heart squeezing in his chest. "Saw who?"

"Moros," she said, rubbing her hands over her face as if trying to wipe away the memory. "He was there... in my dreams. He kept saying... saying that I would cause the end of everything. That I was the reason he was going to destroy all of us. It's all my fault. All of this."

Dante's jaw clenched. He wanted to tell her it wasn't true, that she wasn't responsible for any of this, but the fear in her eyes stopped him.

"What else did he say?" he asked, his voice tight.

Amy's hands trembled slightly as she lowered them to her lap. "He kept calling me Pandora, over and over. And he said that I wouldn't be able to stop it. That no matter what we do, it's too late."

Dante reached for her hand, gripping it tightly. "We're halfway there. Maybe it's just a matter of time now. Whatever happens next, I won't let anything happen to you. I promise."

Amy didn't respond immediately. She stared down at their entwined hands, her brow furrowed as if she was trying to make sense of everything.

Dante's heart pounded in his chest. He hated seeing her like this—scared, uncertain. But there was one thing he knew for sure. "We can stop this. I'm not going to let anything happen to you. You and I, we've come too far. We're stronger together."

Amy nodded, though the worry in her eyes remained. She lay back down beside him, and he wrapped his arms around her, pulling her close.

As the night wore on, Dante stayed awake long after Amy had drifted back into a fitful sleep. He stared up at the ceiling, his thoughts churning with everything that had happened. His powers, their reincarnations, the threat of the gods, and now Amy's nightmares—it all felt like an impossible burden.

Chapter Fifteen

After her first nightmare, it was difficult to fall back to sleep. Listening to Dante's even, slow breathing helped. However, her next dream unfolded slowly, like a fog creeping over a field, distorting reality. She was no longer in the temple or on Delos. This time she stood in an endless expanse of darkness. In the distance, the moon hung ominously low in the sky, its light pale and sickly, casting long shadows across the desolate landscape.

The earth beneath her feet trembled, and when she looked down, cracks began to snake across the ground, splitting the world apart. She could hear the deep rumble of the planet groaning, as if the very core of the earth was ready to explode. She heard screaming then, then a deafening sound, and she glanced up just in time to watch as the moon shattered, like it was being ripped apart by invisible hands. Pieces of it floated away in slow motion, glowing fragments of rock drifting through the sky like fireflies. But it wasn't beautiful—it was terrifying. The pieces began to fall towards the earth, and she could feel the impending doom.

Each fragment seemed to pulse with destructive energy, streaking down like flaming meteors.

Amy's heart pounded in her chest as she tried to scream, to call out, but her voice was gone. She watched in helpless horror as the first fragment struck the ocean, sending waves as tall as mountains towards the land. In their path was a river of fire and smoke shooting up into the sky. The next piece hit the mountains, shattering them into dust. Cities crumbled as more fragments rained down, entire civilizations wiped out in mere moments.

She could hear it then, screaming. Not from the people below, but from the world itself. The earth cried out in pain, its death throes echoing in the deepest parts of her soul. And amidst the destruction, she saw herself standing alone. Alone and powerless.

Then she realized that the entire scene had unfolded far below her. Her long soft gown floated around her in the night air. When she looked down, her bare toes curled and flexed in midair. Even her hair swirled around her in the breeze as the pieces of the moon continued to destroy the planet far beneath her.

But the dream twisted further, taking her back—back to places and times she had never consciously remembered but knew all too well.

She saw herself standing on battlefields, dressed in ancient armor, with Dante by her side. They had fought together, side by side against the gods, their love a force that bound them in every lifetime. But in each scene, it ended the same way.

Dante would fall.

In one life, Zeus hurled a bolt of lightning through his chest. In another, Hades plunged a sword into his back. In yet another, Athena struck him down with her spear. Then

The Stars

it was Moros who pummeled him with stones and his fists. Each time, she screamed his name, her heart breaking as she rushed to his side, only to feel him die in her arms over and over. The pain was endless, an eternal loop of sorrow and loss.

Amy had felt the weight of his body in her arms so many times, the warmth leaving him as his life drained away. Every single time, his eyes would meet hers, filled with the same unspoken promise of love, and every time she lost him. The gods were cruel, and no matter how hard they fought, no matter what strategies they employed, they always lost. She always lost him.

The sorrow was unbearable. She couldn't save him. In every past life, she had failed. And now, the destruction of the world that she had witnessed—the moon shattering—felt inevitable, as though history was repeating itself once more. The fates were laughing at her, reminding her that no matter what she did, the outcome would be the same.

Her heart ached with the weight of it. She didn't know how much longer she could bear the pain of watching Dante die, of holding his broken body in her arms. She wanted to scream, to rage against the gods, to tear them apart with her bare hands. But she couldn't.

She was helpless.

And then, in the dream, as the world crumbled around her, she stood alone again, waiting for Dante to fall. But this time, there was no battlefield. She saw him standing before her, his body twisted in agony, reaching out for her as something dark and unseen wrapped around him, dragging him away.

"No," she whispered, her voice broken. "No, please."

But just as before, he disappeared. She was left alone in the ruins, her heart shattered like the moon.

Amy woke with a start, her body trembling. Her skin was damp with sweat, and she could still hear the distant echoes of the destruction, still see the way the moon had torn apart the sky. Her breath came in short, uneven gasps, and it took her several long moments to remember where she was.

At that very moment, she realized that she was no longer in the soft bed with Dante's body pressed up against hers. The cool salt air floated around her, as it had in many of her dreams.

She had to blink a few times before her mind would understand that she was hovering more than two hundred feet above the dark sea. The stars twinkled above her head, far higher than the massive sliver of the moon that sat in the night sky.

"What..." she whispered, afraid that if she made any sudden moves, she'd fall to earth.

"Sister."

She glanced up and saw two being hovering a few feet away from her. She recognized both of them immediately, somehow.

Venus and Aphrodite. Venus was a pale-skinned woman with long flowing jet-black hair. Her eyes were like diamonds that sparkled in the night. Aphrodite was the most exquisite creature she'd ever seen. Not man nor woman. Long flowing blonde hair the color of gold moved around a flawless face. Eyes the color of the moon and just as bright.

Both were dressed similarly to the long cream-colored night dress she'd been given that first night.

"Sister?" She frowned.

Venus smiled. "Why have you 'forgotten who you are?"

The Stars

"I'm told that if I remember, all will be lost," she pointed out.

"Lies of men can weigh heavy on your soul," Aphrodite said in a rich, soothing voice.

"Are they lies?" she asked. "Prometheus's words and the memories of my life, they all haunt my visions."

"You have been shown what you needed to see to conquer," Venus answered. "Elpis awaits your orders. Once you awake fully, the truth and the hope will finally be released."

"Hope," Amy sighed. "How can there be hope?"

"If not for hope, then all is lost," Aphrodite said.

Amy tilted her head. "Is this real?"

They both smiled. "Is anything real?" Venus asked.

"Love is real," Aphrodite countered. "You feel it in your bones. Every time you watched your mate perish, you lost a piece of yourself until you forgot who you were. What you were fighting for. It's time to wake up. To remember. Love for your mate is the catalyst. It always has been."

"Sister." Venus nodded. Then the pair of them moved so quickly towards her, she had only to blink and they were on either side of her.

"Wake," Venus said, brushing her lips across Amy's.

"Wake," Aphrodite said, and then once more Amy's lips were kissed.

Pain shot through her body as she was engulfed in a bright light. She closed her eyes as it consumed her.

"Remember," they both said as everything burst into flames.

What seemed like minutes passed by as she learned to relax into the pain, accepting it and the images and memories flashing behind her closed eyelids.

When the pain and the light dimmed, she opened her

eyes and realized she was alone and, to her great surprise, still floating above the dark sea.

Looking around, she spotted a few small fires in the distance and pointed her body towards them. Thankfully, whatever flying power she possessed, she didn't need the manual to control it. She zipped through the air quickly towards the campfires, which were obviously on the outskirts of the town.

She spotted the temple where they'd been exiled and, without a sound, she touched down on the balcony.

The room was dark, the only light coming from the faint sliver of moonlight filtering through the curtains.

She swallowed hard as she made her way back into her room, her throat dry and tight as if she'd been screaming. Her pulse was still racing in her ears, a dull, frantic drumbeat that refused to slow. She stilled for a moment after stepping fully into the bed chamber, her eyes adjusting to the dimness.

Then her gaze locked onto Dante. He was still sound asleep, his chest rising and falling in a steady rhythm, his features peaceful. In the darkness, he looked almost otherworldly—strong, powerful, and so much more than the man she had known him to be. But there was something tender in the way his brow softened as he slept, something vulnerable that tugged at her heart.

She watched him for what felt like an eternity, her heart aching with the memory of all those lifetimes, of all the times she had watched him die. She wondered if he dreamed of those same battles, of the pain and loss they had endured together. Did he know how many times he had sacrificed himself for her? Did he remember the way they had fought for a future that never seemed to come?

She reached her hand out, brushing lightly against his

arm, and for a moment she hesitated. She didn't want to wake him. He looked so peaceful, so free from the burdens of their past. But at the same time, she wanted to pull him close, to hold him and remind herself that he was still here—that this time, maybe things could be different.

Tears pricked at the corners of her eyes as she crawled back into bed and wrapped him in her arms. The fear of losing him again was overwhelming.

But even as it threatened to consume her, there was a small flicker of hope. Dante was still with her. They had another chance, another life, another opportunity to change things. Maybe, just maybe, this time would be different.

Amy let out a soft, shaky breath, her hand lingering on his arm. "I won't let you die this time," she whispered, the words barely audible in the stillness of the night. "I love you too much."

As she lay there, watching him sleep, the weight of their past lives, their future battles, and the fate of the world kept her from falling back to sleep.

She would fight for him, for them—for a future where they wouldn't have to say goodbye anymore.

When the sun started to lighten their room, Dante rolled over, his eyes sliding open slowly.

"Morning,'" he said as his hands moved over her.

"I can fly," she blurted out.

He blinked a few times and then sat up. "Okay," he said slowly. "In your dreams, you mean?"

She shook her head as she sat up next to him. "No, last night. I... met Venus and Aphrodite. About a mile offshore." She motioned towards the balcony.

He ran his hands over his face. "Are you sure you weren't dreaming?"

"You glow blue and fought off a god," she pointed out.

"Okay." He nodded. "God, why can't there be any coffee here?" He rolled his shoulders. "Have you tried to fly again?"

She stood up and without exerting any effort, lifted off the ground until her head almost touched the ceiling.

"That is sooo...."

"Cool?" She smiled down at him.

"Hot." He wiggled his eyebrows. "What else can you do?"

Amy floated above the floor, her head just inches from the ceiling, her body weightless and perfectly balanced, as if she'd been doing this her whole life.

"Hot?" she teased, looking down at him, his grin contagious. She wiggled her fingers and did a little twist in the air, her hair floating around her face like she was suspended underwater. "That's all you've got?"

Dante let out a low chuckle and leaned back against the bed, crossing his arms as he studied her. "I mean, it *is* pretty hot. But seriously... what else?"

Amy drifted back down slowly, her feet gently touching the cool floor again. She took a deep breath, the sensation of floating still tingling through her. "I don't know," she admitted. "I haven't thought about it. I feel as if something inside me has been unlocked."

Dante raised an eyebrow, leaning forward slightly. "Unlocked or awakened?"

Since she didn't have an answer, she shrugged.

"Okay, you said Venus and Aphrodite like you're on a first-name basis now," he said.

Amy sighed, running a hand through her hair. "They appeared to me... out over the water. They spoke to me about the past and the future. About hope. About... us."

Dante was silent for a moment, his gaze thoughtful. He

The Stars

rubbed the back of his neck, the tension in his shoulders visible. "So, we're still both pieces in the gods' cosmic chess game." His voice held a dry note, but she could see the wheels turning in his head.

"Feels like it," Amy muttered, pacing across the room. Her mind raced as flashes of last night's encounter replayed in her head. They had spoken to her like she was one of them. A goddess. She could still feel the pulse of energy they'd left inside her, thrumming just beneath her skin.

"I don't know what I'm supposed to do with this power," she admitted, her voice soft. "I don't even know if I want it."

Dante stood and crossed the room to her, taking her hand in his. "We'll figure it out," he said, his voice steady. "You've always been able to get through the tough spots. This isn't any different."

His words settled her, grounding her amid her swirling thoughts. She squeezed his hand, grateful for his presence, even though everything felt like it was spiraling out of control.

Amy studied his face, the determination there unmistakable. She wanted to believe him, wanted to trust that this time would be different. But the memories of her dream, of watching him die over and over again, clung to her heart like thorns.

"There's something else," she said, her voice dropping. "When I was out there... with them... I saw something."

Dante's brow furrowed. "What did you see?"

Amy hesitated, unsure how to explain the strange vision that had flickered through her mind. "I saw... the world breaking apart. The moon was shattered again, the earth crumbling. As it had in the future I'd been to."

His grip tightened on her hand.

"It felt like a warning. We have to get back, somehow, and once I fully understand all of my powers, I have to wake Elpis." She shook her head slightly. "Your sister."

Dante's eyes searched hers for a moment. "Then we need to figure out how to stop it."

She nodded, her mind racing. "But first... we need to understand our powers."

Dante let out a breath and looked towards the balcony where the early morning light was beginning to filter in. "It sounds like we need a place to train." He smiled.

"Yeah," Amy said softly, glancing at the sky. "But first, I need breakfast and some of that tea to wake me up." She paused, the next thought forming before she could stop it. "I can fly."

Dante broke into a grin again. "Well, that's a pretty handy skill, I'd say. Wanna give me a lift next time we need to go anywhere?"

Amy laughed, the sound breaking through the tension between them. "We'll see," she teased, stepping back as she floated just an inch off the ground, testing the sensation. It felt effortless now, like breathing. She wondered what else she could do, what other powers lay dormant inside her.

But for now, she felt lighter. Not just physically, but emotionally. She wasn't alone in this. Dante was here, by her side, and whatever was coming—whether it was destiny, the gods, or the end of the world—they would face it.

As she hovered in place, she caught Dante's gaze, the glint in his eyes unmistakable.

"So," he said, his voice playful, "you're telling me I've got a flying goddess for a girlfriend?"

Amy smirked, lifting herself higher until she was at eye level with him. "Better than a glowing god for a boyfriend, I guess."

The Stars

Dante laughed, shaking his head. "Yeah, I guess we're quite the pair."

Amy touched his cheek gently. "I realized something else last night."

He met her eyes, his hand covering hers. "Oh?"

"I love you." She brushed her lips across his. He stilled and when he pulled back slightly, he was smiling.

"I've loved you for longer than there have been stars," he whispered. Then he kissed her again.

Chapter Sixteen

A few hours later, they stood in the center of the arena theater, facing one another. Amy had tied one of the dresses she'd been provided into makeshift pants. Since their original clothes had vanished, they had to make do with what they had to practice. She tied his tunic into shorts that would keep him covered better than before.

He stood in the center of the ancient arena, feeling the rough stone beneath his bare feet as the midmorning sun climbed higher into the sky. The heat settled on his skin, but it was nothing compared to the surge of energy he felt coiled within him, simmering just below the surface. Across from him, Amy was stretching her arms, her pants cinched tightly at the waist, giving her the freedom to move. She looked focused, but there was a glint in her eye, a spark of excitement he hadn't seen before.

He grinned at her. "You ready?"

Amy returned the smile, rolling her shoulders. "Let's see what you've got, glowing boy."

Dante chuckled, remembering how just yesterday they

had discovered the glow that surged through his body when he tapped into the strange, godlike power within him. His skin had pulsed with a soft light, his muscles brimming with strength. It was like nothing he'd ever felt before, and judging by the way Amy had watched him, she was impressed.

"Don't hold back," he said, lowering himself into a defensive stance. "We need to push each other."

"Wasn't planning on holding back." Amy winked, then launched herself forward, faster than he'd anticipated.

She moved like lightning, her fist aimed directly at his chest. Dante braced himself, feeling the air shift around him as her blow connected. The impact was strong—stronger than he expected—but instead of crumpling, his body absorbed the force, his skin glowing faintly as he deflected the blow with ease.

Amy's eyes widened. "You didn't even flinch."

He shrugged, feeling a surge of confidence. "I guess I'm tougher than I thought."

But Amy wasn't done. She moved again, faster this time, circling him with graceful, fluid steps. Dante followed her movements, his eyes locked on her. She feinted to the left, but before her real attack could land, he saw it—just the slightest shift in her body—and blocked her strike with his forearm.

Amy grinned, impressed. "You're good."

"Thanks," he said, panting slightly, but the truth was, he could feel himself getting stronger with every movement. The more they pushed each other, the more he understood the power inside him. And Amy, well, she was learning too. She wasn't just fast; she had strength that matched his own, and something else... something that gave her the edge in a fight.

The Stars

Every time he struck out or shifted to block her, she countered his moves.

"You're reading me," Dante said, realization dawning. "You know what I'm going to do before I do it."

Amy nodded, wiping a bead of sweat from her brow. "It's like I can see what is going to happen... a second before it does. Not all of your moves, but enough to stay ahead."

"That's... incredible." He hadn't even realized how much she'd been anticipating his strikes until now.

"You're not so bad yourself," she replied, circling him again, her bare feet moving silently across the stone floor. "But don't think that means I'm going to go easy on you."

"Wouldn't dream of it," he shot back, bracing himself for her next move.

Amy lunged at him again, and this time Dante was ready. He deflected her strike, then ducked as she swung a kick towards his head. She was fast, but he was stronger, and when he caught her leg mid-kick, he spun her around and gently—yet firmly—tossed her back a few feet. Instead of landing on the ground with a thud, she floated high up in the air before landing on her feet, gracefully.

"That's new," she said, her breath heavy. "You've gotten stronger."

Dante felt the power coursing through him, the glow of his skin more pronounced now. It felt natural, like this was how his body was meant to be. "I think I can do more," he said, a smile tugging at his lips. "Wanna find out?"

Without waiting for a reply, he launched forward, his fist aimed towards her side. Amy dodged it, barely, her eyes widening as she realized just how fast he'd moved. But instead of backing down, she took to the air in a graceful leap that carried her several feet above him.

"I can fly, remember?" she called down, hovering just out of his reach.

Dante looked up at her, his mind racing. How was he supposed to fight someone who could fly? But then, an idea formed. He crouched low, his muscles coiling like springs, and with one powerful leap, he shot into the air after her.

Amy's eyes widened in surprise as he reached her level, their eyes meeting for a split second before she shot higher, laughing. "Didn't think you could jump that high!"

Dante landed back on the ground, rolling his shoulders. "Neither did I. You wanna come down here and fight, or are we calling it?"

Amy floated back down, her bare feet touching the ground once more. "Alright, alright. No more tricks."

They faced each other again, both of them breathing heavily, but neither willing to stop. Dante could feel the heat between them, not just from the fight, but from something deeper. They were discovering more about each other with every move, every hit, every block.

"You've got more in you," Amy said, stepping closer, her eyes locked on his. "I can feel it."

"So do you," Dante replied, his voice low. "We're not even close to done, are we?"

Amy shook her head, a determined smile on her lips. "Not even close."

They stood there for a moment, both of them buzzing with the energy that pulsed between them. Then, as if by unspoken agreement, they charged at each other again, their bodies colliding with a force that reverberated through the arena. Birds scattered from their hiding spots as a wave of power pulsed each time they connected.

For hours, they fought like that, pushing each other to the brink of their newfound powers. Dante discovered

The Stars

that not only could he withstand Amy's blows, but he could also deflect them with an almost impenetrable force field. His skin seemed to harden with the glow, making him nearly invincible. Amy, on the other hand, could anticipate his every move, dodging and weaving around him like a dancer, her feet never touching the ground for long.

As the sun began to set, they finally stopped, both of them panting and grinning like idiots.

"I think we might be ready," Amy said between breaths, her hands resting on her knees as she looked up at him.

Dante nodded, wiping the sweat from his brow. "Yeah. I think we are."

They stood in silence for a moment, the enormity of what they'd just discovered settling in. Whatever was coming, they were ready to face it—together.

"Come on," Dante said, reaching out his hand. "Let's go back before it gets dark."

Amy took his hand, squeezing it tight. "Lead the way, glowing boy."

They walked out of the arena, side by side. They were more than just human now. They were something stronger, something bigger.

As they made their way through town, they both sensed something was off.

"Where is everyone?" Amy asked him, looking around.

Then they heard the shouts and followed the screams to the water's edge.

"What has happened?" Amy asked a woman.

"The gods, they are angry with us." She motioned to the water.

In the distance was a wave the size of a mountain.

Dante's first thought was that it was a tsunami.

"Wait." Amy grabbed his hand. "Look. The water. It's not moving."

He shielded his eyes and sure enough, the wave hovered almost a mile off the shore.

"Should I go see what's happening?"

"Only if you can take me with you," he countered.

She glanced around. "Do you think we'll freak them out?"

He shrugged. "They already think we're gods."

She nodded and then frowned. "I guess we should have practiced how I would carry you when flying."

He stepped towards her and wrapped his arms around her body. "Let's try this. If you drop me, I'll only get wet," he pointed out just before they lifted off the ground.

Sure enough, only a few of the townspeople gasped or cried out at the sight of them flying away.

It took a few moments for them to adjust their hold on one another, making the flight more comfortable. Amy didn't fly like in the old Superman movies, horizontally. Instead, she darted through the air upright, which, thankfully, made it easier for Dante to hold onto her. The wind whipped through his hair as they soared over the waves, the distant shoreline growing smaller behind them.

"There," Amy said, pointing at a small form surrounded by the water below them.

When they got closer, Dante squinted and realized it was a small figure trapped in what appeared to be a giant air bubble, floating atop the dark sea.

"Theo!" Amy gasped, her grip tightening on Dante's arm as she almost lost focus. Her body faltered midair for a split second, but she quickly steadied herself.

Dante leaned forward to get a better look, his heart pounding in his chest. Below them, the small boy was curled up in the bubble, crying. His shoulders shook with silent sobs until Amy screamed his name. He looked up, and his tear-streaked face lit up with a smile as he saw them hovering over him.

"I knew you'd come," Theo said, standing shakily within his bubble prison as he wiped the tears from his eyes. "He said you wouldn't."

"Who?" Amy asked, flying closer.

A dark, rumbling voice broke through the air before Theo could answer. "Finally..." it said, the sound seeming to come from the depths of the ocean itself. "I've found you."

"Moros?" Amy whispered, fear rippling through her words. A figure rose from the water, dark as shadow and as cold as death. "Thanatos," she breathed in horror.

Every muscle in Dante's body tensed as his instincts flared to life. The light from his body surged, his power roaring in response to the god's presence. Amy's own light flared alongside his. Together, their energies combined in a burst of radiance that shot directly at Thanatos.

The god of death smiled darkly, barely flinching as he raised one hand and flicked Amy's attack away like a mere fly. "I see that it's true," he said, his voice dripping with mockery. "You have woken, Pandora."

Dante growled, and before he thought about it, he pushed forward in midair as if preparing to strike, unaware that he was now flying. His power surged even brighter, and for a moment, Thanatos hesitated, his dark eyes narrowing as he studied Dante more closely.

"And Epimetheus," Thanatos murmured, his voice low with recognition. "This is a surprise. It seems most of your powers have returned as well." He smirked. "Haven't quite mastered how to fly on your own yet?"

Without warning, Thanatos launched forward with

terrifying speed, his dark form cutting through the air towards Amy. Dante's reaction was immediate—he stepped in front of her, his arms raised in defense, bracing for impact. The power that burned within him reacted instinctively, a shield of blinding light forming around him. Thanatos's blow slammed into it, sending shockwaves through the air, but the shield held firm.

"Not today," Dante growled, pushing back against the god's strength.

Thanatos snarled in frustration, his dark energy swirling around him like a storm. He attempted to strike again, but Dante's shield flared brighter, repelling each blow with increasing intensity.

Amy, her body trembling with the effort to stay in control, shouted, "Theo! Hold on!"

While he fought off Thanatos, she flew downward in a blur, her hands reaching out towards the boy's bubble. With a burst of her power, the bubble shattered, releasing Theo from his prison. He fell directly into her arms, gasping with relief.

Thanatos stopped mid-assault, his dark eyes narrowing as he took in the scene before him. A slow, eerie smile curled across his lips.

"Once again," he said, turning back to Dante, who hovered effortlessly over the dark waters, his power radiating, "together, you are far stronger than we anticipated. But next time we meet, you will fall—together, as always."

With that, he vanished into the mist, leaving behind nothing but an ominous echo of his laughter. Dante's body still buzzed with adrenaline as he turned to Amy, who was now cradling Theo in her arms.

"Are you okay?" Dante asked, his voice rough with the aftermath of the battle.

Amy nodded, her breathing heavy but steady. "He's safe now." She motioned towards him. "I guess you can fly too."

He glanced down at himself and smiled. "Yeah, guess so." Then he looked at her. "Do I look as cool as you do?"

"Even better." She laughed.

As they floated back towards the shore, Theo whispered in Amy's ear, his eyes wide with wonder, "Thank you, Pandora... Epimetheus... for saving me."

Dante clenched his jaw. They were no longer just Amy and Dante. They were something more—something that even the gods feared.

And now, there was no turning back.

Chapter Seventeen

By the time the three of them landed safely back on the beach, the crowd had grown in size and everyone was chanting their names. Their god names.

Everyone gathered around them, cheering and hugging Theo. Moments later, the water separated a few feet from the crowd as Prometheus stepped out from the sea.

"I see you disobeyed the gods," he said to Dante. "Well done." He smiled and slapped him on the shoulder before turning towards Amy. "Sister," he said with a quick nod. "Welcome back."

"Is this it then?" Dante asked. "Will you send us home now?"

Prometheus chuckled. "I was not the one who brought you here."

"But you can send us back, right?" Amy asked.

He turned fully towards her. "No, sister. You are the only one here with that power."

"Me?" Amy was shocked. "I... I..." She shook her head.

"You are the one who came here, to him,"—he motioned

towards Dante—"on your own powers. You are immortal and omnilingual, as with all gods. Your knowledge surpasses even mine." He waved his hands slightly as if convincing her. "You've been known, in the past, to create weaponry out of thin air."

"I have?" She looked down at her hands and willed a dagger to appear. Sure enough, moments later an intricate silver blade with a bright yellow stone on the tip of its hilt appeared. She'd had visions of this knife before. Seen her past self-wielding it in battle.

"Cool," Dante said, getting her attention.

"No, sister, it is not I who will send you to your next step in your journey." Prometheus bowed his head slightly. "I am out there in your time, waiting for your arrival and awaiting my fate." He glanced at Dante. "As it has always been, I will stand beside you both when the time comes for the final battle. It is up to you, Pandora, to ensure that the last piece is in place to finally end this game." He glanced down at Theo. "Well done, boy." He winked at the kid, then turned and walked back into the sea.

Amy's mind swirled as Prometheus disappeared into the sea, the waves closing in as if he'd never been there at all. His words echoed in her mind—*You are the only one here with that power.* Her?

Immortality, omnilingualism, the power to create weaponry from thin air. Could she do all of that?

She thought about how she could easily understand the ancient Greek everyone spoke around her. How she could read the writing on the temple walls. Then she realized that even though she'd been reborn, that was, in a way, immortality.

Dante stepped closer, placing a hand on her back. "You okay?"

"I... I don't know," she admitted softly, her eyes still fixed on the spot where Prometheus had vanished. Everything was happening so fast. The gods, the power inside her—powers she had barely scratched the surface of. And now, to learn that *she* was the one responsible for getting them home.

Dante gave her a reassuring smile. "Hey, we've gotten this far. We'll figure it out. Besides, I can fly." He wiggled his eyebrows and she laughed.

His calm confidence steadied her, and she took a deep breath. She squeezed the hilt of the dagger she had just conjured, marveling at its weight and craftsmanship. *How had she done that?*

Thinking quickly, she held out her other hand and a thick leather strap appeared. It matched the dagger perfectly, and when she slipped the blade into it, she knew that this too was hers for all time.

"Pretty cool," he said as she wrapped the thing around her waist.

Theo, still beaming from the rescue, wiped at his eyes and turned to her and Dante. "Thank you," he said quietly, his small voice lost in the sea of cheers.

Dante ruffled the boy's hair, grinning. "You did good, kid. I think you were a lot braver than we were."

Amy bent down to meet Theo's gaze, her heart warming at the sight of him safe and sound. "You were really brave," she said softly, her hand resting on his shoulder.

Theo smiled again, his youthful face brightening. "I knew you'd come for me," he repeated, like a quiet, steady mantra. Amy's chest tightened at the faith this boy had in them—in her.

The villagers led them back to the village, where a feast

was quickly put together. Large wooden tables were brought out to the center of the square.

They sat at the head table under arches of flowers and decorations the villagers had hurriedly strung up. Music filled the air, joyous and celebratory, as the smells of roasting meat and bread wafted around them.

It was almost surreal, like something she'd seen in a movie. The entire village had turned out to honor them, to praise them as gods. They'd barely wrapped their heads around their identities as Pandora and Epimetheus, and yet here they were, celebrated and revered. It was a strange, heady feeling.

The villagers talked about how they had not only saved Theo but the entire town. If they hadn't stopped Thanatos, he would have destroyed everything and everyone there.

Amy supposed that it could be true. From what she could remember of the myths, Thanatos would have wiped the entire village from history without blinking an eye.

The feast stretched on for hours—dancing, laughter, and an endless flow of food and something close to wine. Amy tried to join in, smiling and nodding as villagers approached her with gifts and words of thanks, but her mind was far away, still turning over Prometheus' parting words.

You are the only one here with that power.

As the sun began to dip below the horizon, her exhaustion finally caught up to her. She exchanged a glance with Dante, who seemed equally drained.

"Ready to head back?" Dante asked, leaning in close so only she could hear.

She nodded gratefully. "Yeah, I think I've had enough 'godhood' for one day."

They quickly said their goodbyes before making their

The Stars

way back to the temple. The familiar sight of the ancient structure brought a strange comfort to Amy—it was the closest thing they had to a home in this strange world.

As they entered, the sounds of the feast still faintly carried on the breeze, but here, in the quiet of the ancient stone walls, Amy could finally breathe again. She sank down onto the bed and ran her hands through her hair, still processing everything that had happened.

Dante sat beside her, stretching out his legs and letting out a long sigh. "Today was... something."

"Yeah," Amy agreed, her voice barely above a whisper. She stared at the ground, her thoughts a whirlwind of power, gods, and responsibility. How could she control all of this? Could she truly figure out how to use her powers to get them back home?

Dante must have sensed her anxiety, because he placed a hand on her knee, giving it a gentle squeeze. "Are you okay?"

She nodded and leaned into him, resting her head against his shoulder. "I'm just... scared. I don't know if I can get us home."

Dante wrapped an arm around her, pulling her closer. "You can," he said firmly. "I have faith in you. Like Prometheus said, you have the power. You made that." He motioned to the knife that sat beside her on the bed.

"Yeah." She smiled slightly. "I didn't even really have to think about it."

"So maybe the power to take us back is like creating the dagger?" he suggested.

She shook her head. "No, I've tried several times to just think about taking us back."

"And nothing?" he asked, and she nodded. "Maybe..." he started but then stopped.

"What?" she asked after a moment.

"Well, maybe you don't want to go back?" he surprised her by saying.

"I..." She stood up and walked over to look out over the water as the truth bubbled inside her. He was right. She didn't want to go back to a world she knew would soon be destroyed.

He moved behind her and when his arms wrapped around her, she leaned back against his chest.

"It is peaceful here," she said softly. She glanced up at the moon and felt a shiver race through her. "And the world isn't destroyed or on the verge of it."

The weight of his arms around her was grounding, and for the first time since Prometheus had disappeared into the sea, Amy allowed herself to relax, just for a moment. They stood there in the dimming light, the temple quiet and still, a brief moment of peace amidst the chaos.

But deep down, Amy knew this was only the beginning. The journey ahead was fraught with danger, gods who sought to destroy them, and powers she was only really beginning to understand.

As the last rays of sunlight disappeared behind the horizon, plunging the temple into darkness, Amy closed her eyes and took a deep breath.

"I know it's time to go," she said, taking a deep breath. Then she turned into his arms. "But can we have one last night together here?"

He smiled down at her. "One last night." He brushed his lips across hers. In that instant, her entire body reacted almost as much as it had when they'd been in danger. Every fiber of her being was on fire, heated, as his hands ran over her.

In the past few nights together, they'd explored one

The Stars

another until there was an invisible connection holding them together. Cosmic strings that defied time and space bound them together.

Tonight, somehow, everything was different. The knowledge that this might be the last night of peace they would have had their movements slowing. The passion built until an urgency spilled over and the speed fed their desires.

"My god," Dante whispered as he hovered over her. "Where have you been my entire life," he said with a grin.

She ran her fingers through his thick hair. "Right in front of you."

"Amy, I know I've said this to you a few times now, but" —his eyes locked with hers—"I love you."

Her smile was quick. "You have said it a few times and I know it's true. Each time, we've loved like this."

He shook his head. "No, this time is different."

She frowned slightly. Could it be different this time?

The thousands of times he had told her how he'd felt in past lives played in her mind. He'd told her that he loved her more times as she'd watched him die.

This did, however, feel different. Maybe because she was here, now. Or maybe because she wanted it to be different.

"I hadn't expected the frown and that sexy little crease right here." He touched her forehead. "Not the response I'd hoped for."

She relaxed her face. "Just remembering all the other times we said those words to each other in our past lives." She shook her head. "I love you. And most importantly, I would love to hear you say it a million times again."

He chuckled. "I suppose for someone like you, who remembers all those times we've said it to one another, this isn't the most romantic time."

She cupped his face and brought it down to hers until his lips were inches from her own.

"This is the most important one to me," she whispered before they kissed.

Amy woke a few hours later, her heart pounding in the stillness of the night. The soft rise and fall of Dante's breathing beside her was the only sound in the room, a steady rhythm that grounded her amidst the whirl of emotions swirling inside her. She blinked, slightly disoriented, and glanced towards the window. The moonlight filtered in through the open balcony doors, casting a soft glow over the temple's stone walls.

For a moment, she stayed still, listening to the quiet, but something pulled at her—a deep sense that this was not just another sleepless night. Quietly, she slipped out of bed, careful not to wake Dante. His arm slid off her waist as she moved, his warmth lingering on her skin.

She grabbed her long gown from the floor and pulled it on as she padded barefoot across the cool stone floor towards the balcony. The soft night breeze carried the scent of the ocean, and the horizon was a dark, endless stretch beyond the cliffs. She leaned against the railing, her fingers gripping the cool stone, and gazed out at the sea. The world felt so still, but her mind was racing.

How did we even get here?

The last few days had been a blur of ancient gods, powers she never imagined, and the discovery that she and Dante were bound together in ways deeper than anything she could have anticipated. And now, as they prepared to return to the future, she couldn't shake the feeling that something crucial was missing—something she needed to do before they left this ancient world behind.

Suddenly, her vision blurred, and the world around her

The Stars

shifted. It was as though time itself was bending. Amy gasped, gripping the balcony as her mind was pulled into another place, another moment.

She was back in Hidden Creek. The familiar scent of pine and earth filled her senses as she stood on the edge of town, watching herself from the future—her *other self*. The one who had been left in the hotel room after Ryan had broken things off suddenly. After which, she'd returned home, broken, but had decided to stay in Hidden Creek, and because of that, she'd ultimately found her way to Dante.

However, in this vision, Ryan didn't break things off and they returned to town together as planned. They had stayed at her parents' place for less than a night and had fought the entire time before returning to the city together. She hadn't met Mia. Hadn't rented the little cabin, flirted with Dante, or gone to Xtina and Michael's place that fateful night. Which meant... she glanced back at Dante's sleeping form and returned to the vision quickly when the entire world exploded without her even fighting for the chance to save it. She'd been at work in Atlanta, blissfully unaware of what was about to happen.

Then, the vision changed, and this time she stood outside the hotel room—the one she and Ryan had stayed in just before everything changed. She was wearing the long nightgown that she was currently in. She watched herself move over to where Ryan was sitting on the stairs, smoking. As she sat next to him, she reached out, touched his hand, and knew that if she didn't break things off with him, none of what she'd just gone through in the past few months would ever happen.

She had a choice.

To live in ignorance with Ryan, a man she didn't love,

until the world was destroyed or to love Dante and fight with him to the very end.

I have to do this.

If she hadn't made this choice—if she hadn't traveled forward and broken up with Ryan—none of what had happened would come to pass. She and Dante would never have been reunited. The future would shift, their bond severed by a choice not made.

Amy's heart clenched, and she closed her eyes and willed her body back to that fateful night at the hotel when she felt the power surge through her like electricity.

When she opened her eyes, she smiled as she stood just outside her hotel door.

Inside, she knew that her past self was sound asleep, blissfully unaware of the storm that was about to break.

Ryan sat a few feet away, his back to her, sitting on the stairs just outside their room, staring down at his phone as he smoked. He was unaware that she'd just traveled through time and had appeared out of thin air.

When she stepped forward, he glanced up, obviously startled when she walked towards him. His face softened in confusion, the boyish smile she had once desired flickering across his face as his eyes ran over her long gown.

"I thought you were asleep," he said. "New getup?" He chuckled.

She sat next to him with a shrug. "I couldn't sleep," she said truthfully, ignoring the comment about her gown. He probably wouldn't remember that detail when he left in the morning, because she had still been under the bed covers when he rushed from the room.

She hesitated, her heart constricting at the knowledge of what came next. Her entire future, hers and Dante's future, depended on what she did next.

The Stars

"Ryan," she began, her voice barely a whisper. She cleared her throat, trying to steady herself. "We need to talk."

He blinked, his brow furrowing in concern. "What's going on? You look... upset."

She shook her head, tears pricking at the corners of her eyes, but she forced them back. "I—I care about you, Ryan. I always have. But... things have changed. I've changed. And I need to be honest with you."

His face fell, the realization dawning on him. "Amy, what are you saying?"

"I'm saying that this"—she gestured between them—"isn't right anymore. I'm not the person I was when we met. I'm... different. I need to be somewhere else, and I need to be with someone else." She swallowed hard, the words catching in her throat. "I'm so sorry."

He stared at her for a long moment, his face a mixture of hurt and confusion. "Is there... is there someone else?"

Amy's chest tightened. *Dante.* The name echoed in her mind, but she didn't speak it aloud. She simply nodded, the weight of her confession hanging in the cool night air.

Ryan's expression hardened, the pain evident in his eyes. He stood, pacing a few steps away, running a hand through his hair. "I... I don't understand. After everything we've been through, after all this time, you're just... dumping me?"

"I have to," she said softly. "I'm sorry, Ryan. I am. I know you're tired. Please, get some sleep before you head home in the morning."

There was a long silence, broken only by the distant sounds of cars passing by on the highway. Finally, Ryan let out a shaky breath and nodded, though the sadness in his eyes cut her deeply. "I guess I can't stop you, can I?"

Amy shook her head, tears finally spilling down her cheeks. "No."

He sighed, his shoulders slumping in defeat. "I hope... I hope you find whatever it is you're looking for."

She wanted to say more, to explain everything, but the words wouldn't come. So she simply stood up and turned as if to walk back into their hotel room. His eyes stayed glued to the cigarette as she melted and returned through time.

She had done it. The choice was made, and the path was set. Now she could return to Dante.

Once more she was standing on the temple's balcony, the cool night air brushing against her tear-streaked cheeks. She inhaled deeply, her chest heavy with the weight of the choice she had made, but also lighter, knowing that it had been the right one.

She turned and quietly slipped back into the room, her gaze falling on Dante's sleeping form. He was lying on his side with his face relaxed as the moonlight cast soft shadows across his features. This time, her heart ached with the love that she felt for him. She knew that her choice, the pain that she'd put herself through, was worth it—every painful moment, every heartache, was to get her back to this moment.

She slipped back into bed beside him and sighed when her body fit perfectly against his. Dante stirred slightly but didn't wake as she listened to his steady heartbeat and knew that the love she felt for him was beyond any cost she had paid in the past.

As the first light of dawn began to creep through the windows, Amy closed her eyes, knowing that whatever the future held couldn't be stopped.

Chapter Eighteen

Dante blinked as the world around him shifted, the golden hues of the ancient temple vanishing in an instant. His heart raced, and for a brief moment he felt disoriented.

When everything stilled, his eyes darted around, searching for any sign of where—or when—they were.

They had decided to leave after the morning meal and after they'd freshened up. It was midmorning before they had stood on the balcony and wished the beauty and the serenity of that peaceful world goodbye.

Now the familiar scent and heat of Georgia hit him, and he realized with relief that they were back in Hidden Creek.

The giant cover of the silo loomed high above them. He knew that it was the same place and time when Brea had sent them away. A few candles flickered in the corners, casting shadows across the gathered faces. Everyone was still there, frozen in surprise as if they hadn't noticed Dante and Amy had been gone for what felt like days. Everything was the same as when they'd been whisked away. Had only seconds passed here?

Amy's hand tightened around his, her breath catching as she looked around the room. Dante felt her tension shift, a sharp intake of air, and he followed her gaze to where Joe and Liz stood. Joe's arm was protectively around his wife's waist.

"Joe!" Amy's voice broke the silence, excitement bubbling up inside her as she darted forward, releasing Dante's hand. "Liz—oh my god!"

Joe's eyes widened in shock as Amy ran up to him, practically tackling him into a hug. "What—what just happened?" Joe stammered, bewildered. "You just left, and then—"

Amy laughed, pure joy in her voice, cutting him off. "I'll explain everything, but first—triplets!" She pulled back and placed her hands on Liz's large belly as she beamed with excitement. "I know that you and Liz are having triplets!"

Liz, who was standing beside Joe, blinked in surprise. "Wait, what? How do you know—"

Amy clapped her hands together, practically bouncing on her toes. "Long story, I'll explain later! But I saw them, met them—the triplets! Congratulations!"

Joe looked utterly confused but a smile tugged at his lips as Liz, still processing, placed a hand on her belly. "We haven't even told anyone, we wanted it to be a surprise."

Everyone around them watched the exchange and since she'd just spoiled their surprise, everyone gathered around them and congratulated Joe and Liz on the news.

"What's happened? How did you see them?" Xtina asked.

"Seriously, so much to tell you all!" Amy replied breathlessly, glancing back at Dante, as if to share her excitement.

The Stars

Dante smiled at her, feeling the warmth radiate from her joy. Her reunion with her family felt like the first peaceful moment they'd had in days. But the weight of everything they'd experienced—the gods, her visions, their new powers, the ancient prophecies—it all still pressed heavily on his mind. And now they had returned to a world that had barely noticed they were gone.

How much would it change now that they were back?

"Dante!" Jacob's voice cut through his thoughts. He turned to see his boss walk over and shook his outstretched hand. "Welcome back, I guess." He chuckled. "Nice digs."

Dante glanced down at his tunic and groaned. "Yeah, I'm desperate for a change of clothes and a cup of coffee."

Michael jumped in and said, "How about we head back to our place? You can both change and fill us in on what you've gone through."

"Yeah," Xtina added, her arms crossed over her chest, "and you can tell us why you're both so tan and practically glowing. What did you do, go on a magical vacation or something?"

Dante chuckled and exchanged a glance with Amy, who was still buzzing. "Something like that," he replied. "We were... uh, in the past. Like, ancient Greece."

Jess jumped in as she raised an eyebrow. "You what now?"

Amy finally pulled herself away from Joe and Liz and rushed back over to where Dante was standing.

"It's a long story," she said, her voice still filled with excitement, "but we were sent back in time—like, way back. We met Prometheus, met the three Fates, and... and fought off a god, sort of."

"You saw the Fates?" Mia asked. "Did you understand anything they said? What did they say?" she added quickly.

"Lots," Amy sighed. "No, not really, but I guess, now we do understand what they told us." She shrugged.

"You guys are okay though?" Jacob asked as they all started making their way out of the silo.

Dante nodded, still feeling the residual energy from the godlike powers he'd awakened. "Yeah, and we've been fighting gods for many lifetimes. Like we said, it's a lot to take in."

"Okay, so you time-traveled, met some gods and the three Fates, and now you're back with suntans and new clothes. That about sum it up?" Mia said as they climbed the stairs in a single line.

Amy laughed, her energy contagious. "Pretty much. And that's not even the craziest part."

"We've got powers now," Dante added, glancing down at his hands as if the glow might still be there. "It's... hard to explain, but we've unlocked something," Amy said.

"Pandora is awake?" Mia asked.

Amy nodded slowly. "I guess so since I can remember all our past lives."

"What sort of powers?" Mia asked after a moment of silence.

"I'm really strong. I can create weapons from out of thin air. I can understand any written or spoken language. I can see an opponent's moves before they make them. I'm immortal. Oh, and I can fly," she said, matter-of-factly. "We can fly," she corrected. "Dante... well, he's really strong and kind of invincible now."

Michael let out a low whistle. "Damn. That's some next-level superhero shit."

Dante smiled, but there was a weight behind his words as he added, "It's not all fun and games, though. There's more going on—big things. We've got a lot to figure out."

Amy's expression sobered a bit as she nodded in agreement. "We were told that the final battle is coming, and we're going to need all the help we can get. We need two more people if we're going to win."

"Who?" Jess asked.

"Elpis," Mia and Lucas answered together.

Dante and Amy glanced at them. "How did you know?"

"Only Elpis can stop Moros," Lucas answered.

"And Pandora will waken Elpis when it is time," Mia added. "We too visited the Fates," she added dryly.

"Right." Amy nodded.

At least no one thought they were crazy. He and Amy might have been the ones chosen by the gods, but they weren't in this fight alone. They had their friends and their family. They had a team.

The group stepped out finally into the field above the silo and its underground hidden mazes of rooms and chambers.

As they headed back towards Xtina and Michael's house to regroup and talk through everything, Dante hung back for a moment. He glanced at Amy, who was laughing with her brother and Liz. He enjoyed seeing her smile, which was wide and so full of life. At that moment he felt an overwhelming sense of peace.

They were back. And together, they were ready to face whatever came next.

Then Jacob slapped him on the shoulder. "Why don't you fill me in quickly as we walk?"

For the next fifteen minutes, as they made their way across the dark field, he gave his boss, who was also one of his best friends, the rundown.

By the time they stepped into the house, Jacob and a few others, including Lucas, Michael, and Joe, were all caught up since they had walked together. The rest of the group had followed Amy closely as she talked quickly about some of the visions that she'd seen.

Thankfully, Michael and Xtina gave them a change of clothes. Once they were out of the ancient attire, they all gathered in the living room with a fresh pot of coffee and they filled everyone in on what they'd discovered.

He was grateful for the warm, familiar clothes and space, not to mention the smells and taste of freshly brewed coffee. He and Amy both enjoyed two cups along with some freshly baked cookies Jess had made.

As Amy explained the rest of what they'd gone through, Jacob sat at the table, leaning back in his chair with his arms crossed. Lucas stood by the window, staring out with a pensive expression, while Joe hovered near the coffee pot, refilling mugs. The rest of the group sat around listening, hanging on every word they said.

Amy was very animated as she caught everyone up. She spoke with urgency and determination.

Dante sat on the couch next to her and added bits to the story where he could. The relief of finally being back in regular clothes helped him relax.

The gods weren't just an abstract danger—they were real, and they were coming. Soon. He looked at Liz, knowing that they only had a month after the triplets were born.

"Okay," Xtina said, clapping her hands together to get everyone's attention. She stood by the coffee table, her sharp gaze sweeping over the room. "Let's break this down. Amy, you said the gods are going to attack a month after Liz gives birth to the triplets?"

"October tenth," she said with a frown as she leaned forward. "Joe told me." She glanced over at her brother. "I

The Stars

was sent ten years into the future, long after..." She shook her head. "You told me that Moros and Thanatos will lead the charge."

Joe let out a long breath, his hand resting protectively on Liz's shoulder as she sat beside him.

Dante noticed that Amy didn't mention the fact that Liz would die in that first wave and that Joe would be left to raise the triplets alone or that, in ten years, everyone in the room would die as well.

The room fell into a tense silence, everyone absorbing the gravity of what they were up against. Dante could feel it in the air, the unspoken fear, but also a shared resolve. They'd faced danger before, but this... this was different.

Michael leaned forward, resting his elbows on his knees. "So what exactly are we up against? We need details."

Amy's eyes flicked over to Dante, and for a moment, he felt the warmth of their connection surge between them. She turned back to the group, her voice steady despite the weight of her words. "It's not just Moros and Thanatos. There will be others—minor gods, creatures... Harpies. We're going to have to rely on our powers, all of our powers, to stop them."

"Seriously? Harpies?" Jess shook her head. "Do we even know what all of our powers are? I mean, we know most of our abilities, but have we really explored yours? What about Elpis, once she arrives or awakens?"

"Elpis is my sister Hope," Dante broke in and several people in the room gasped.

"Seriously?" Mia asked, slightly shocked.

"Yes," Amy agreed. "I've seen her and talked to her. Well, Elpis at any rate. She was Hope but... not." She shook her head.

"Like when I met you as Pandora first and then met Amy." Mia smiled. "I get it. We've been so worried about finding the pair of you, I never figured we'd get lucky that someone here would already know her."

"How do we get her back in town?" Jacob asked.

Amy nodded. "We need to figure it out—and fast. Dante and I... we've been learning things about our abilities. We're stronger together, but we also need everyone else. All of us will have a part to play. First, however, we need to get Hope back in Hidden Creek and find Prometheus."

"I'll handle that," Dante said quickly. "We've seen Prometheus's physical form, so it will be easy for Amy and me to spot him," he pointed out.

"Then what?" Lucas asked. "Do you know how hard it was for Mia and me to keep from telling Amy who she was?"

"You can't tell them who they are," Amy said. "Just like Mia knew what to do, I'll know when and what to do to help Elpis and Prometheus take their paths."

Dante took a deep breath. "Amy's right. We've faced these gods before in our past lives, but this is on another level. Something tells me that this is the end game. These gods, they're not just going to come at us with brute force. They'll play with our minds and twist our realities. We need to be ready for anything. And we need to be united."

"Yeah, but how?" Ethan asked from where he sat, Brea's hand resting lightly on his arm. "We don't even know what they'll throw at us. And how the hell do we fight multiple gods? We pushed Moros and Thanatos back when they attacked individually, but how are we supposed to do it when they come at us united and with an army of..."

"Harpies," Jess and Amy finished for her.

Amy crossed her arms, her expression fierce. "We fight

them the way we've fought everything else—together. Our powers, our bond, our connection... that's what gives us an edge. We just need to train, to prepare."

Selene, who had been quietly listening, spoke up. "Amy's right. I can feel it. We're not just fighting them physically. This will be a battle of wills, of hearts. They'll come after what we hold most dear."

Colt jumped in. "We have already started by figuring out exactly what each of us can do. We've been training every week. We'll add Amy and Dante to our sessions. Then we'll strategize. If we're stronger together, we need to learn how to combine all of our powers."

Lucas shifted from where he stood at the window, his arms crossed over his chest. "And we'll need a plan. Now that we know when they're attacking, we need to make sure Liz and the babies are safe. Along with the rest of the kids."

"The silo," Amy jumped in. "It's where everyone goes. We need to fill it with food, water, necessities. It's our stronghold. At least..." She stopped and shook her head.

"For a while," Dante finished for her.

The room grew quiet. Everyone seemed to understand what he was saying.

"Then we'll start there," Jacob said as he stood up.

Dante glanced at Joe, who was frowning, his jaw clenched tight. Liz's hand was resting on her growing belly, her expression tense but resolute. She met Dante's eyes and nodded, determination flickering in her gaze.

"We'll be ready," Liz said softly. "Whatever happens, we'll be ready."

Amy smiled at her sister-in-law, pride and affection in her eyes. "We will. And we're not alone in this. We have each other, and we have allies. Prometheus said others would stand with us when the time comes."

"Prometheus," Xtina said, raising an eyebrow. "Prometheus gave fire to humanity."

"Yep," Amy replied, leaning back on the couch, her arms crossed. "He's our brother and has been guiding us... sort of. Like I said, he and Elpis are..."

"Mated," Dante finished as he took Amy's hand in his. "Like the rest of us are."

Brea shook her head in disbelief. "Okay, so let me get this straight. We have a month to find and wake Elpis and Prometheus, figure out how all of our powers can work together, train, build an underground shelter, and then prepare for an epic god showdown. No pressure."

Dante chuckled softly, the tension in the room easing a bit as Brea's sarcasm lightened the mood. "Amy has seen that we've faced worse in past lives," he said with a grin, but deep down, he knew this was going to be unlike anything they'd ever experienced.

As the group began to strategize, discussing training schedules and potential defenses, Dante caught Amy's eye. Her smile was small, but it was filled with the same fierce determination that had carried them through everything so far.

And as he looked around the room—at his friends, his family—he felt a swell of hope. They would face the gods together. And they would win.

Chapter Nineteen

It was all so hard to wrap her mind around. Once everyone was caught up on the past week of their lives, Amy and Dante stepped out of the front door of Xtina and Michael's place.

She leaned against Dante as they stood together, the night air far chillier than the past few nights they'd enjoyed. The stars above Hidden Creek glittered brightly, and for a moment, she let herself just breathe it in—the familiarity of being back home after what felt like weeks, though it had only been days.

"I never expected to miss this place." She sighed.

"Makes you appreciate everything more," he agreed.

Her eyes fell on their cars parked among the others, like nothing had changed. The sight was oddly comforting, grounding her in the reality that, despite everything, they were back, safe.

"How is it possible?" she murmured, staring at the cars. Hers was exactly where she'd left it days ago, in her mind. "Everything's exactly where we left it."

Dante's hand found the small of her back, his touch

steady and reassuring. "It's like we never left," he said softly, his voice warm and full of the same disbelief she was feeling.

It was a little past two in the morning.

"What next?" he asked.

"I think you mean, your place or mine?" she joked.

His hands moved up and down her body. "Your place is fine. I'm sure you want to get into your clothes and sleep in your bed."

"Your place is bigger," she pointed out. "I can stop by my place first and grab a bag of things. It's on the way."

He grinned, the moonlight casting shadows across his face as his hands rested on her waist. His lips brushed hers, soft and teasing. "Whatever you want," he whispered against her mouth. "Just as long as I get another night holding you."

She smiled up at him, her arms slipping around his neck as she leaned into him. Being with him now, after everything they had just gone through, it felt like the most natural thing in the world.

Amy's heart fluttered at his words, the sincerity in them making her stomach flip. There had been so much between them—uncertainty, distance, timing. But now? Now there was clarity. A certainty that she belonged with him, in every possible way.

They walked together to her car, the world around them still and quiet. The night felt thick with possibility, and even though the gods' threat still loomed over them, for this moment, everything was perfect.

She leaned against her car door, her hand still intertwined with his. "I never thought it would feel this... normal."

Dante chuckled softly, his thumb brushing over her

knuckles. "After everything we've been through, normal feels pretty good, doesn't it?"

She nodded, biting her lip as she stared up at him. "I don't want this to end. Us, I mean."

His eyes softened, his free hand brushing a strand of hair behind her ear. "It won't," he promised. "Not now, not ever. We've found our way to each other so many times. That's never going to change."

Her heart swelled at his words, and for the first time in a long time, the future didn't feel so terrifying. It felt... hopeful.

"Then let's go home," she whispered, leaning in to press her lips to his. The kiss was soft but full of promise, and as she pulled back, her heart pounded with the knowledge that she had finally found her place.

Half an hour later, she glanced over at Dante as he drove his truck up the steep grade of his driveway. They had quickly swung by her place and he'd waited as she'd packed an overnight bag with some essentials.

After having nothing for almost a full week, it seemed strange to toss makeup and other toiletry items into a bag. She threw in some jeans and shirts along with the sexiest clean underwear she could find in her dresser drawers.

She decided to keep her car at her place and jumped in his truck to ride with him over to his house.

Somewhere below them in the dark, Hidden Creek was asleep and it felt like the world belonged to just the two of them. Every now and then, Dante would glance at her, a smile playing on his lips. She could feel it—the comfort of being with him, the weight of what they had gone through lifting, if only for a little while.

As they approached the top of the hill, Dante slowed down.

"Home sweet home." He sighed as his headlights landed on the place.

Amy couldn't see much of his property in the darkness, only the faint outlines of trees and the distant shimmer of the river. Dante's place sat higher up, secluded but with what she knew would be a stunning view.

His home was a beautiful two-story white cabin with a black metal roof that gleamed faintly in the moonlight. There was a recent addition of the large wraparound deck that circled the front and side of the house. A detached three-car garage sat a little way off, its outline barely visible in the shadows. She'd heard how much he'd done to the place over the years. Joe had helped him put the roof on shortly after he'd purchased the place.

It felt so right—like she belonged here. It wasn't just the home itself, though she had always admired the simple, rustic beauty of it. It was being here with him. That's what made it feel like someplace she could finally call home.

Dante parked the truck and stepped out, coming around to her side to help her with her bag. "I've got it," he said, tossing her bag over his shoulder.

"Thanks," she said, taking his free hand as she slid out of the car. "I forgot how beautiful it is up here." She glanced around the property. "Even at night, you can just feel the peace."

"Wait until morning," Dante said, his voice warm as he closed the car door behind her. "You'll see the river, the trees... it's one of the reasons I bought the place. That view."

He led her towards the house, his hand never leaving hers, and as they stepped onto the deck, the wood creaked softly beneath their feet. "I like the new wraparound porch."

The Stars

Dante chuckled. "It took longer than I expected to finish it, but it's perfect for morning coffee, trust me."

They walked to the front door and, once inside, the warm, earthy scent of wood greeted them. The cabin's interior was simple but cozy—high ceilings with exposed beams, wooden floors, and soft lighting that made the space feel intimate and inviting.

The rich wood flooring was covered with a few thick rugs in places. He had dark leather furniture with rustic tables and lamps, and stunning nature art hung on every cream-colored wall.

There was a large stone fireplace in the living room, and from what she could see, an open newly remodeled kitchen off to the back of the building.

It was everything she imagined his home would be—practical yet charming, with little touches of him everywhere.

She felt his hand at the small of her back as he led her towards the staircase that wound up to the second floor. Her heart skipped a beat when his arms slid around her waist, lifting her effortlessly off her feet.

"Dante!" she gasped, laughing as she instinctively wrapped her arms around his neck. "What are you doing?"

"Carrying you up," he said simply, his eyes gleaming with mischief. "Because I can."

She shook her head, grinning as she held onto him, her face nestled against his neck. "You're ridiculous."

"Maybe," he murmured as he started up the stairs, each step slow and deliberate. "But I like taking care of you. Besides I've always wanted to carry someone up these stairs."

The staircase was perfect for it. It was wide enough and, with a slight curve, romantic enough.

Her chest tightened at his words, warmth spreading through her as he carried her up to the main bedroom. When they reached the top of the stairs, she glanced around, catching a glimpse of the space—the wide, open room with a king-sized bed and large windows.

Dante set her and her bag down gently, his hands lingering at her waist for a moment before he kissed the top of her head. "Welcome to my humble abode."

Amy smiled, leaning into him. "It's perfect." She meant it. More than the house, more than the view—being here with him made everything feel right.

She turned to face him, their gazes meeting in the soft glow of the bedside lamp. For a long moment, they just stood there looking into one another's eyes.

"I'm glad we're here," she whispered, her hand sliding up to cup his cheek. "Together."

Dante leaned down, brushing his lips softly against hers. "Me too. Amy?" he said against her lips.

"Hmm?" she purred.

"I'd kill for a shower."

She laughed. "You read my mind." She dropped her arms. "Tell me your shower is big enough for the both of us."

He laughed and nodded as he took her hand in his.

A few minutes later, they stood together under five powerful showerheads blasting hot water at them from all different directions.

"This is heaven." She sighed as she leaned into the powerful jets.

"Tell me about it." He rolled his shoulders.

She closed her eyes, letting the hot water work its magic

on her tense muscles. The steam rose around them, cocooning them in warmth and silence. The jets of water felt like they were washing away not just the dirt and sweat from their long days but the weight of everything they had been through. Everything that had led them to this moment.

She moved closer to him, her wet skin sliding against his. He opened his eyes and she smiled up at him, droplets of water clinging to his lashes as she tilted her head up. "You look like you're in bliss," she teased, running her hands over his shoulders, her touch gentle but firm.

"I am," he admitted, his voice low and content. He reached up and tucked a wet strand of hair behind her ear. "It's been a hell of a few days."

She nodded, leaning into his hand as he cupped her cheek. "I know... but we're here now." Her fingers traced the lines of his chest, leaving a trail of heat in their wake, despite the water cascading over them.

He pulled her closer, his arms wrapping around her waist as he pressed his forehead to hers. "That's all that matters."

For a moment, they just stood there, the water pounding around them the only sound in the room. The world outside felt far away, as though it didn't matter—at least not in this moment. Here, it was just the two of them, finally able to breathe, to relax, to be.

Amy's hands slid up to his neck, her fingers playing across his shoulders. "So... about that bed," she murmured, a playful smile tugging at the corner of her lips.

He chuckled, leaning down to capture her mouth in a slow, lingering kiss. "We'll get there," he whispered against her lips. "But I'm in no rush."

She had never experienced sex in a shower before and was thankful for the shower seat and the pebble tile flooring for grip. Not to mention Dante's strength in keeping them from slipping and falling.

"That was a little dangerous," Amy joked as they stepped out and wrapped towels around their bodies.

"I'm thinking of installing a few handholds for safety." He laughed as she started to dry her long hair.

"I know it's probably three in the morning, but I'm still wired." She slipped on a tank top and shorts she'd brought in her overnight bag.

She glanced over and watched him pull on a pair of gym shorts. God, he was amazing, everything she'd ever wanted throughout all time.

"Want to see what I have in the kitchen?" he suggested.

"I am dying for something with refined sugar in it." She laughed.

A few minutes later, they sat in his living room watching television while eating any junk food that he had in the house.

It was by far the most normal thing they had done all week and one of the best times that she'd had in her entire life. They laughed together over old shows until they finally fell asleep in each other's arms on the sofa.

The next morning when his alarm went off, he groaned.

"Sorry," he mumbled. "I'm forgot that I'm scheduled to work today." He rolled off the sofa and searched for his cell phone somewhere in the house.

"That reminds me," she said, sitting up. "I should charge my phone. I need to share the photos of the writing from the temple with the others today. We're meeting for coffee at eleven."

She ran her hands over her face while he turned off his alarm.

"I'll try to make it." He glanced at the time and winced.

The Stars

It was hard shifting their minds back to normal life. "I've got to get going. I'll drop you back off at your place."

She stood up and nodded. Seeing the look in her eyes, he quickly moved over to wrap his arms around her. "I'd love for you to pack up more than just an overnight bag. I don't want you to go."

She smiled up at him. "Did you just ask me to move in with you?"

He chuckled. "Move in with me," he said softly.

"Okay," she sighed and then kissed him.

"You're sure?"

"Very sure." Her heart jumped in her chest. "Dante, we go beyond time and space. It's not going to be easy to get rid of me."

He hugged her. "Thank the gods." He sighed into her hair. "I love you."

"I love you," she replied as his second alarm went off.

He groaned. "Tonight," he promised her. "We'll have a proper first dinner together in our home."

"I like the sound of that."

Chapter Twenty

Amy stood at her cabin door, keys in hand, looking at the small place she had called home for less than two months. It felt surreal to pack up her few belongings, knowing that she was moving in with Dante.

She opened the trunk of her car and carefully stacked the last of her things inside. She wasn't surprised at how little she had. Once she and Ryan had called things off, she'd left most of her old things in the city. She'd taken only what she could fit in her car after Joe had driven her back to her small apartment to get her things. She had wanted to start fresh when returning home and now she was thankful for it.

Funny, she'd been so broken over Ryan breaking up with her back then. Now, of course, she realized that technically she was the one who had called things off.

With one last glance at the cozy cabin, she drove off, excitement and nervousness swirling in her chest. As she drove into town, the beautiful fall colors surrounded the roads, making her nostalgic for her favorite season of the year.

Fall in Hidden Creek was stunning. The bright orange and red leaves covered the trees and roads. There were signs of the coming Halloween season everywhere. Homes and businesses were decorated with fun skeleton scenes or seasonal flare, even though it was a little over a month and a half away still.

When she pulled into the Coffee Corner, she could see that Xtina, Jess, Mia, Brea, and Liz had already gathered, talking and laughing at a table by the window. The moment Amy walked in, they waved her over.

"Amy." Jess grinned and pushed a cup of coffee towards her. "Your favorite. How was your first night back?"

"Thanks, it was wonderful." She took a sip of the coffee. Jess had a strange power to know what everyone wanted. Then again, she was a witch and the owner of the coffee shop.

As they sat down, Amy pulled out her phone. "Okay, so you won't believe this. But I got photos of our trip. I forgot to show everyone last night because my phone was dead and, well, there were a lot of other things going on." She scrolled through the pictures she had taken of the mountain temple, the carvings, the statues, everything. She passed her phone around the table, and their eyes widened as they flipped through the photos.

"That's insane," Mia breathed, staring at the intricately carved walls. "This is... ancient writing and a temple, right?"

Amy nodded. "Yeah, it was surreal. The carvings, the architecture... all of it."

"What does any of it say?" Xtina asked, looking down at the phone.

"You can't read it?" she asked.

"No," Xtina said, along with the others.

"I guess I'll have to translate all of it." She paused, biting her lip.

Xtina furrowed her brow. "You can read all of this?"

"It's part of the powers we unlocked," Amy explained, leaning in. "Prometheus said I have omnilingual abilities. Apparently, all gods and demi-gods do. I'll need to spend some time translating what each of these says."

The group was quiet for a moment.

"Who is this?" Liz said, turning the phone around to show a picture she'd taken with Theo when he'd told them about the temple.

"That's Theo." Amy smiled. "A boy who helped us while we were there."

"Theo?" Xtina frowned.

"Yes." Amy quickly ran through what had happened, how the boy had found her on the side of the mountain and taken her into town. How he had helped them find the temple and then how they had saved him from Thanatos.

"Of course," Jess said, snapping her fingers as she picked up her own phone and typed something in. "Theogony." She smiled and turned her screen around to a sketch of an older Greek man. "In the 7th century BCE, Theogony wrote several epic poems titled 'Days by Hesiod.'" She paused. "The story of Pandora and Epimetheus."

"What? Seriously?" Amy took Jess's phone and quickly scanned the page. "Wow, way to go Theo." She laughed.

"We wouldn't have most of the stories of the Greek gods if not for him," Jess added.

"Fate," Liz said softly. Everyone glanced over at her. "Sorry." She ran her hands over her large belly. "Being an oracle has some drawbacks." Her eyes scanned everyone's. "Knowing that the birth of my children starts the ball rolling for the end of the world... I've always known, but I had hoped that something would change."

"It still can," Amy said, taking her sister-in-law's hand in hers.

Before anyone could respond, Liz suddenly inhaled sharply, clutching her stomach. Her face paled, and her wide eyes met Amy's. "Oh my god."

"Liz? What's wrong?" Brea asked, concerned.

Liz's breaths were shallow, and a nervous smile tugged at her lips. "I think... I think my water just broke."

The table erupted into chaos, everyone scrambling to grab their things and help Liz get to the hospital. Amy's heart raced for a brief moment, knowing that the moment had finally arrived—Liz's triplets were finally coming.

The hospital was buzzing with an undercurrent of excitement and tension as Amy, Mia, Xtina, Jess, Brea, and the others gathered in the waiting area. The anticipation of Liz giving birth to triplets—Luna, Stella, and Orion—had the entire group on edge. Joe had met them there at the hospital after she'd called him and told him what was going on, and he and Liz had been whisked away into delivery, leaving everyone anxiously waiting for news.

The sterile, bright lights of the hospital hallway showcased everyone's nervous smiles. She could see it on everyone's faces, time was running out.

The hours passed slowly, and the conversation dipped in and out of normalcy, though there was an unmistakable sense of urgency in the air.

As night settled in, Dante and Jacob finally arrived after work, their expressions shifting to relief when they saw everyone still waiting.

The Stars

"Any news?" Jacob asked, rubbing the back of his neck as he walked over to Jess, who was sitting on the edge of her chair.

"Not yet," she answered, smiling softly up at him. "But I think we're getting close."

Dante walked straight over to Amy, placing a gentle hand on her shoulder. "How's Liz?"

"She's strong," Amy replied, leaning into him. "We're all just waiting now."

The hospital cafeteria was the only place open at this late hour, so they all decided to grab some hamburgers while they waited. The group moved into the brightly lit cafeteria, settling at a long table. The sound of trays clattering and muted conversations filled the space as they all sat and ate.

Amy pulled out her phone again, scrolling through the photos of the temple. She hadn't been able to stop thinking about it, and it was clear that something significant was connected to the carvings and text.

"I showed these to a few this morning, but I've been meaning to show the rest of you something," she said, glancing around at the group. "These are from the temple Dante and I found. It's our story."

She handed her phone to Tara, who was sitting closest, and soon it made its way around the table. As the images of the ancient carvings were passed from person to person, Amy noticed something unusual. Tara paused, studying one of the photos with a slight frown, and then passed it to Selene, who did the same.

Joleen and Lucas shared a glance before Lucas spoke up. "How is it that I can read ancient Greek?"

Amy's heart skipped a beat. "Wait, you can?"

Tara nodded, her voice quiet but certain. "I can too. These symbols, the stories in them, they're familiar."

Selene leaned in, tapping one of the images. "These are the writings of the gods. Somehow, I know them."

Joleen chimed in. "We're all demi-gods, remember? Our heritage runs deep."

Amy blinked in surprise. She hadn't fully connected who was a demi-god and who wasn't. "So the four of you can translate these?"

Lucas nodded. "Yes."

They all exchanged glances, the realization settling in. They too had an army of gods for the fight.

Dante, who had been silent until now, crossed his arms. "We need to figure out what these stories mean as soon as possible. If they're just past lives or if there is a warning about the future in any of them."

"Agreed. Send us copies of these images. We can all go over them and look for clues," Lucas suggested.

The moment Liz's triplets were born, they knew that Moros and Thanatos wouldn't be far behind. The clock would start ticking, and the countdown would officially be started.

They returned to the waiting area and, less than an hour later, Joe came out with a huge grin on his face.

"Mom and all three babies are doing great," he said to cheers.

Then he showed them all the photos of Luna, Stella, and Orion. The babies were all snuggled in colored blankets with little hats on their tiny heads.

"When can I see them?" Amy asked her brother.

"Tomorrow. Liz has asked that we get rest for tonight," Joe responded.

After Joe returned through the doors, everyone dispersed in silence.

While they were joyful about the new life, a shadow of

impending danger loomed over them all. They had one month to convince Hope to return to Hidden Creek and to find Prometheus.

An hour later, Dante held her in his arms as they snuggled in his bed together. His hand gently traced circles on her shoulder blade.

"I called my sister today," he said softly.

"And?"

"She'll be here tomorrow. I told her Dad was having some health issues."

She sat up and looked down at him. "You lied to your sister?"

He nodded with a grin. "To save the world? You bet."

"What about Prometheus?" she asked, laying her head back on his chest.

"Let's just hope that whoever he is, he is somewhere close by." He sighed. "For now, at least, Hope is on her way."

Oddly, it wasn't as difficult to fall asleep as she'd expected. Not with the clock to the end of the world already ticking. When exhaustion finally took over, her dreams were filled with the faces of her two nieces and nephews. How they had been or would be ten years from now. Their laughter and smiling faces filled her visions.

Thankfully, for the first time in days, her dreams didn't turn dark. She woke with Dante's alarm and decided to head down to the hospital early to see her new family. She dressed and drove out of their driveway moments after he did.

After a quick stop for coffee and a short shopping spree, Amy arrived at the hospital carrying a bouquet of soft pink lilies for Liz and three small, carefully wrapped gifts in her arms. The hospital halls were brightly lit but quiet in the early morning.

Stepping into Liz's room, she was greeted by the warm, sleepy smile of her brother standing beside Liz's bed. Her sister-in-law was cradling one of the three newborns in her arms. Joe's grin widened when he saw her.

"Morning," Joe said softly, careful not to wake the babies.

Amy gave him a quick hug and then walked over to look down at the three tiny bundles.

"I can't believe they're here. Congratulations," she whispered, placing the flowers on the small table by Liz's bed. "They're all so perfect."

She sat down gently on the edge of the bed, her eyes immediately drawn to the three babies, each swaddled in pastel blankets.

"These are for them," Amy said, handing the bag with the small packages inside to Liz, who carefully unwrapped them. Inside were delicate silver charms—one shaped like a crescent moon for Luna, a star for Stella, and a tiny constellation for Orion.

"They're beautiful, Amy," Liz said, her voice full of emotion. "Thank you."

Amy smiled warmly, then glanced at Joe. "I couldn't resist. They'll be able to wear them when they're older." She remembered seeing them around each child's neck.

Earlier, when she was making her way through town and had stopped to get Liz flowers, she stopped by chance at the antique store. When she spotted the charms, she knew instantly that she was the one who had given them to the children.

Liz chuckled lightly. "You don't have to spoil them already."

The Stars

Amy shrugged playfully. "That's what aunts are for."

For nearly an hour, she visited, holding each baby in turn. Luna with her sleepy eyes, Orion who squirmed in her arms, and Stella, so calm and peaceful. The world outside faded away as they all savored this new chapter in their family's life.

Eventually, Liz yawned, exhaustion settling in again from lack of sleep. Amy stood up, brushing a hand through Liz's hair affectionately. "You rest, okay? You've earned it."

"Thanks," Liz smiled, her voice barely above a whisper.

Amy stepped out of the room and began walking down the hallway. It wasn't often she got to feel this calm, especially after everything she'd been through lately.

But just as she neared the hospital's exit, the calm was shattered. The doors burst open and Dante rushed through them as he helped guide a gurney. His uniform was rumpled, and his face was a mixture of worry and focus. He rushed beside the team that was wheeling the gurney towards the ER. Suddenly, Amy's heart dropped.

"Dante?" she called, moving towards him, concern etched on her face. He didn't seem to hear her at first, his attention fixed entirely on the unconscious woman being rushed inside.

Hope.

Amy recognized Dante's sister immediately—her dark hair and face were covered with blood, there was a deep gash on her forehead, and her rich dark skin was now ashen.

"She was in an accident." Dante's voice was strained as he finally met Amy's gaze, his eyes pleading. "We got the call. A car hit hers head-on on the highway just outside of town... I don't know how bad it is. She's been unconscious this entire time."

Without thinking, Amy followed Dante as he trailed

behind the ambulance team. They were quickly stopped by a nurse just inside the ER doors. "I'm sorry, you'll have to wait here."

Dante's frustration was palpable, but Amy gently squeezed his arm, trying to ground him. "They'll take care of her," she reassured him softly, though her own heart raced.

Just then, a figure rushed past them into the exam room that Hope had been wheeled into, and Amy's breath caught in her throat as the doctor jumped into action to work on Hope.

The doctor was tall and tan, with sandy blond hair and crystal silver eyes. He even had the sexy stubble on his chin and the dimples. There was no doubt. They had just found Prometheus.

Dante's eyes also widened in disbelief as the man, dressed in scrubs, stepped forward with calm authority, his gaze immediately falling on Hope. He quickly assessed the situation, his hands already working, giving directions to the nurses and other doctors.

"What the hell?" Dante whispered, barely audible.

Amy couldn't answer. She was just as shocked.

Everything was finally in place.

Just in time for the end of the world.

Also by Jill Sanders

The Pride Series
Finding Pride

Discovering Pride

Returning Pride

Lasting Pride

Serving Pride

Red Hot Christmas

My Sweet Valentine

Return To Me

Rescue Me

A Pride Christmas

The Secret Series
Secret Seduction

Secret Pleasure

Secret Guardian

Secret Passions

Secret Identity

Secret Sauce

Secret Obsession

Secret Desire

Secret Charm

Secret Santa

The West Series

Loving Lauren

Taming Alex

Holding Haley

Missy's Moment

Breaking Travis

Roping Ryan

Wild Bride

Corey's Catch

Tessa's Turn

Saving Trace

Christmas Holly

Maggie's Match

The Grayton Series

Last Resort

Someday Beach

Rip Current

In Too Deep

Swept Away

High Tide

Sunset Dreams

Lucky Series

Unlucky In Love

Sweet Resolve

Best of Luck

A Little Luck

Christmas Wish

Silver Cove Series

Silver Lining

French Kiss

Happy Accident

Hidden Charm

A Silver Cove Christmas

Sweet Surrender

Second Chances

Dancing on Air

Entangled Series – Paranormal Romance

The Awakening

The Beckoning

The Ascension

The Presence

The Calling

The Chosen

The Beyond

The Void

The Stars

Haven, Montana Series

Closer to You

Never Let Go

Holding On

Coming Home

The Hard Way

Never Again

Pride Oregon Series

A Dash of Love

My Kind of Love

Season of Love

Tis the Season

Dare to Love

Where I Belong

Because of Love

A Thing Called Love

First Comes Love

Someone to Love

Fools in Love

FindingLove

Christmas Joy

Always My Love

Forever My Love

Searching for Love

Wildflowers Series

Summer Nights

Summer Heat

Summer Secrets

Summer Fling

Summer's End
Summer Wish
Summer Breeze
Summer Ride
Summer Affair

Distracted Series
Wake Me
Tame Me
Save Me
Dare Me

Stand Alone Books
Twisted Rock
Hope Harbor
Raven Falls
Angel Bluff
Day Break
Diamonds in the Mud

For a complete list of books:
http://JillSanders.com

About the Author

Jill Sanders is a New York Times, USA Today, and international bestselling author of Sweet Contemporary Romance, Romantic Suspense, Western Romance, and Paranormal Romance novels. With over 100 books in eleven series, translations into several different languages, and audiobooks there's plenty to choose from. Look for Jill's bestselling stories wherever romance books are sold or visit her at jillsanders.com

Jill comes from a large family with six siblings, including an identical twin. She was raised in the Pacific Northwest and later relocated to Colorado for college and a successful IT career before discovering her talent for writing sweet and sexy page-turners. After Colorado, she decided to move south, living in Texas and now making her home along the Emerald Coast of Florida. You will find that the settings of several of her series are inspired by her time spent living in these areas. She has two sons and off-set the testosterone in her house by adopting three furry little ladies that provide her company while she's locked in her writing cave. She enjoys heading to the beach, hiking, swimming, wine-tasting, and pickleball with her husband, and of course writing. If you have read any of her books, you may also notice that there is a love of food, especially sweets! She has been blamed for a few added pounds by her assistant, editor, and fans... donuts or pie anyone?

- facebook.com/JillSandersBooks
- x.com/JillMSanders
- amazon.com/Jill-Sanders/e/B009M2NFD6?tag=jillm-com-20
- bookbub.com/authors/jill-sanders
- instagram.com/jillsandersauthor
- tiktok.com/@jillsandersauthor

www.ingramcontent.com/pod-product-compliance
Lightning Source LLC
LaVergne TN
LVHW041802060526
838201LV00046B/1090